Also by

Shannon Esposito

SAHARA'S SONG

STRANGE NEW FEET

THE MONARCH

LADY LUCK RUNS OUT

KARMA'S A BITCH

(A Pet Psychic Mystery)

A NOVEL

Shannon Esposito

misterio press

Karma's A Bitch

* * * * *

Visit Shannon Esposito's official website at
www.murderinparadise.com

* * * * *

Cover Art by India Drummond

Formatting by Debora Lewis
arenapublishing.org

* * * * *

ISBN-13: 978-1477657942

This book is dedicated to my daughter, Sadie, who so wisely suggested I write something for fun and to those of you who have lost your heart to a pet.

ONE

Our first customer had a wet nose and, as it turned out, major daddy issues.

"Now if I could only get you to stop tinkling in daddy's shoes!" Sarah Applebaum gushed, as her chin got a tongue bath from her newly groomed Shih Tzu. "You just look so precious. He has to forgive you now, right Wizzy Wizzy Lizzy?"

Wow, Sarah could spew some serious baby talk. I censored a chuckle while I rang her up for the grooming; a pink, organic cotton PRINCESS t-shirt and seven gourmet, carob treats. Laughing at our very first grooming client wouldn't be polite—or good business sense for that matter— especially a new customer with about five grand worth of diamonds in her bracelet alone.

"*Essa senhora é demente*," my friend, business partner and groomer, Sylvia, mumbled behind me. I didn't speak Portuguese but, after spending the past month around her, I had started getting the gist of her remarks. I cleared my throat with a smile.

Sylvia was all dark passion, curves and confidence. In one word: exotic. I was a platinum-haired, milky-skinned twig just sticking my toe into society—outside my family—for the first time at twenty-eight. The Shih Tzu wasn't the only one with daddy issues. Anyway, Sylvia and I worked on some level I didn't quite understand but did appreciate.

"Lady Elizabeth giving y'all some problems?" I placed the receipt on the counter with a pen and reached out to stroke a silky brown ear. Sylvia had rocked the grooming, even topped it off with a jewel-encrusted bow holding the dog's bangs out of her eyes. A tiny, pink tongue reached out and licked my hand.

Youch! As the tongue made contact, a prickly current traveled up my hand. With it came an image and the scent of cheap perfume. I felt my face flush, the hair on my arms stand up.

Leaning back, I stared at Lady Elizabeth, who panted and then sneezed, which sounded a lot like, "see!" The energy buzzed around inside me like a swarm of mad bees, the image still glowing hot in my mind.

I glanced at an oblivious Sarah Applebaum and rubbed my nose, even though the sickening sweet perfume smell came from my sixth sense, not my sense of smell.

"We tinkle on the pad, not in the shoes." Sarah kissed one of Lady Elizabeth's fluffy feet and admired her cherry red nails. "I don't know what's gotten into her lately."

I had a pretty good idea but couldn't exactly blurt it out. "Does your husband look a bit like a young Leslie Neilson?"

Sarah Applebaum blinked. "Well, yes, I suppose so. Why?"

"And I don't suppose you have a daughter? Blonde? Fond of black lace?" I said this last part under my breath.

"No. A son, actually. He lives in Texas. Do you know my husband?"

"Oh. No. I um," I tucked an unruly wave behind my ear and glanced at Sylvia for help. But Sylvia just stared at me, arms crossed, dark eyes searching under an arched brow. No help there.

I shrugged. "I must be thinking of someone else." How to get out of this one? I held up a finger. "Hold on a sec, I have something for you to try." I power walked down the aisle, back to the storeroom and flipped on the light. Jumping up and down and running in place, I tried to dispel the energy still coursing through my body. As far as vision-energy went, this was fairly tame but still, I didn't need a repeat incident of the last time.

Sylvia cleared her throat behind me.

"Wha-yow!" I yelled, hopping around and holding my heart. "Don't sneak up on me like that!"

Sylvia grinned, her rich brown eyes sparkling with humor. "What are you doing? Do you need to use the potty?"

"Ha ha. No." I turned back to the shelves in front of her, my cheeks burning. "Just looking for something for Lady Elizabeth." I ran a finger over a row of 30 ml brown bottles with glass pipettes, reading the labels. "Aha...elm, honeysuckle, red clover." I palmed a bottle and pondered the dog's situation. "Probably will need something for her emotional stability." Tapping my chin, I plucked another bottle off of the shelf. "Grey spider flower and chamomile should do it." Spinning around I almost barreled into Sylvia, who still stood in the doorway watching me.

"Some of your magic flower essence for the pee peeing pooch?" Sylvia asked.

"For the pooch, yes." I nodded. "For the pee peeing, no." Then, lowering my voice, I added, "and it's not magic."

Sylvia, who grew up in a large Catholic family, lovingly referred to my flower essence creations as "woo woo" stuff. To me, raised in a house where concocting flower essence was like cooking a family recipe—and really, on the low end of the freaky scale in our house—it seemed as natural to hand out a bottle of flower essence as it would to hand out an aspirin. Although, now that I had fled to St. Petersburg, Florida from my family's Savannah, Georgia home for a chance at normalcy, I realized all the people who had whispered behind our backs and shunned us may have had a point.

"Here you go, Mrs. Applebaum." I wrapped the bottles in pink tissue and placed them in her bag. "It's flower essence. Just squeeze four drops of each on Lady Elizabeth twice a day and massage into her skin. Should help reduce whatever anxiety she's feeling about your husband right now." *And whatever she's going to feel about him in the future.*

"Oh, thank you, Darwin. I'll pass the word to all my friends about how great you gals are." She pressed a tip into Sylvia hand. "So glad you're here now. I'll see you soon!" She lifted the Shih Tzu's paw and waved at us with it as she left.

Sylvia's dark, silky ponytail whipped around with her body. "Spill it, *my amiga*. What was all that about?"

"What was what about?" I pretended to straighten out the one receipt in the drawer.

Before she could respond, the bells hanging on the door signaled another customer.

"Welcome to Darwin's Pet Boutique!" I said, with maybe a bit too much enthusiasm.

"Good morning," the elderly woman, sporting a heavy German accent, replied.

"How can we help you?" Sylvia raised an eyebrow at me. I recognized this as her secret signal that this conversation wasn't over.

"I need to make grooming appointment for my dog, Heidi."

"Certainly."

"Hey, Sylvia," I reached beneath the front counter and grabbed a folder. "Since you've got this, I'm going to walk over to the dog park and hang up our flyer." I pushed out the door and into the sun baked morning before Sylvia questioned me further. I was determined to be normal here and Sylvia's curiosity about the 'woo-woo' stuff could very well threaten that.

Gad! Shielding my eyes, I considered running upstairs for my sun hat. How is it so bright at nine thirty in the morning? I mean, we experienced southern summers in Savannah but here the flat, wide open sky and sunshine pushed summer up to a whole new level of intense.

Instead, I sucked it up and crossed Beach Drive and into North Straub Park. The park was a sprawling, grassy area between the strip of shops and eateries on Beach Drive and the sparkling blue waters of the yacht basin. The iconic Vinoy Renaissance Resort bordered the park on the north, the Fine Arts Museum on the south. A real live slice of paradise pie.

I paused on the sidewalk and just stood there taking in the *view* and breathing in the moist, balmy air, my heart literally light as a balloon. Over the past few weeks, my decision to leave home had gnawed at me. I was fond of Savannah and I did miss my family, but moments like this helped reinforce the notion that I had made the right decision.

It was love at first sight for me and St. Pete. I felt energized, alive and unbound here. I attributed some of it to my sympathetic connection to water, but there was something else, too. The energy here just hummed with possibility, like an adventure waited around every palm tree and peach colored condo.

I stepped onto the grass and made my way over to the shade of a giant banyan tree. There, I spotted a man propped up against the tree's massive, above ground root system. A newspaper lay across his face. Stretched out beside him was a large mastiff, who watched me with a hanging, panting tongue that reminded me of melted silly putty. Approaching him, I reached into my khaki shorts pocket for one of the sweet potato bones I had baked over the weekend. I'm a real sucker for a big slobbery smile.

"Hey, big guy." I leaned down and held out the bone when a hand suddenly shot up and grabbed my arm. "Hey!" I yelped as I found myself pinned down, one arm behind my back in less time than it took me to shout. "Ptt!" I spit out damp sand.

"Oh," the man released my arm and hopped up, helping me up off the ground. "Sorry, ma'am. You caught me off guard." He winced. "I didn't hurt you, did I?"

I eyed him as I rubbed at my mouth and a grass stain on my bare knee. "Good gracious you're a quick one." Then, deciding he wasn't a threat, I straightened up and offered him a smile, holding up the bone. "No. It's my fault. That's what I get for sneaking up on y'all. Just wanted to give your dog a treat. I make 'em. I've got the new pet boutique across the street. Darwin's." I motioned behind me. "I'm Darwin." I held out a hand. "Quite a dog you've got there."

The man glanced at my hand without taking it. I tried not to be offended. "Not really mine. Kind of adopted me. I call him Karma and," his eyebrow shot up, "most people are scared of him." He glanced at the bone and sighed. "He doesn't have teeth but I'm sure he'd be happy to gum it to death."

I laughed and held out the bone in front of the massive face. Intelligent brown eyes stared up at me. "Well go on, Karma. You soften it up enough, it'll go down fine." The mastiff reached out and took the bone gently from my hand and sprawled back out with a noisy *hrmph*. "Good boy." I gave his large head a scratch. No zap. Thank the universe. I couldn't take another jolt so soon. "He doesn't look old enough to have gum disease. What happened to his teeth?"

"Don't know. He's only hung around with me about six months." He kneeled down and lifted the dog's top lip, releasing a stream of drool onto his arm. It didn't seem to faze him. "Has a couple of nubs in the front. My guess? Maybe a rock chewing habit. We've all got our demons, isn't that right, boy?" He patted the dog's rump with a firm hand. The dog's tail thumped the grass.

I checked out the arms loaded with tattoos, the hole in his boot, the dusty t-shirt, the worn back pack against the tree and wondered what kind of demons the man was living with. Was he one of the homeless I had heard were so prevalent downtown? Taking a harder look at the lean frame and dull fur on Karma, I cleared my throat. "Well, I've gotta go get this flyer up at the dog park but," I paused, "I didn't get your name?"

"Mad Dog."

Mad Dog? Definitely not his real name. Who was I to judge, though, with a name like Darwin? "Okay, Mad Dog, remember I'm right across the street. If y'all need anything feel free to visit the pet boutique." I waited until his chin tilted up and locked my gaze with his, so he'd know I was serious. "I mean it, now. Anything...food for Karma or a cool place to get out of the heat."

His head dropped. Was I being rude suggesting he needed help? I'd never met a homeless person before, maybe I was being too forward? Change of tactic. "I'm new here and haven't made many friends yet. I'd love the company." Oh heavens, did that just sound like I wanted a date? Nice, Darwin. "What I mean is, you know, I'm a big dog lover..." Karma stopped gumming the bone and stared up at me, dripping drool, his ears cocked forward. "Yeah, I know." I sighed, shrugging. "What I should say is I'm better with animals than people."

Mad Dog glanced at me out of the corner of his eye and then a soft chuckle stirred in his chest. "Yeah, me too."

TWO

"Good morning, boys an' gals." I slipped on the cheesecloth glove I had crafted so my vibrations wouldn't be added to the pansies' and rested one of the fresh petals between a thumb and forefinger. My eyes closed as a weak quiver tickled my fingers. "Not ready yet?" Okay.

I moved my hand to the next bloom. This one fluttered like a humming bird's wings. Pulling a pair of tiny shears from my yellow gardening apron, I snipped the head off and placed it in a glass bowl of distilled water. Repeating this process, the water's surface was almost covered when I spotted my new friend across the street.

"Mad Dog!" I held my straw sunhat down with one hand and waved with the other. "Good morning!"

Glancing around, he finally spotted me on the balcony above the boutique. I rented this "city home" from Sylvia, who purchased it as an investment with the large sum she inherited when her grandfather died. She said it was a sign from God that it was for sale right above the space we picked out for our pet boutique. I had learned early on in our new friendship not to argue with her.

This was the first place I'd lived on my own and I had to say—the million dollar, three thousand square foot, two story place was a bit overkill for me. It was, however, gorgeous and the perfect location.

Mad Dog held up a hand and I waved him over.

"I'm heading next door for some tea before I open the boutique, would y'all join me?" I called down to him and Karma. Both of them stared up at me, heads tilted. Before he could turn me down, though, I pulled off my glove. "Stay there, I'll be right down." I moved the bowl of flowers to the balcony table and covered it with a square of cheesecloth from my apron. I'd have to remember to retrieve it at lunchtime.

Hurrying back through the French doors, I tossed my sunhat on the couch, grabbed my straw bag and, as an afterthought, slipped into some flip flops. Wearing shoes was one of those things I was still getting used to.

"Beautiful day, isn't it? Hello, Karma!" I exited the tropical courtyard tucked between buildings and pulled the iron gate shut behind me.

"Yes, ma'am. It is. A beautiful day."

I scratched Karma beneath the ears and smiled at Mad Dog. He wore the same dusty gray t-shirt and the same guarded expression. "Shall we?"

We walked to the Hooker Tea Company a few shops down. This had been a big selling point for me when Sylvia and I had scouted out places for the boutique, being the crazed tea fanatic that I am.

"Don't think they'll let Karma come inside, so why don't you grab a table out here and I'll go in and order. Any preference? White, green, black?"

"No, ma'am." Mad Dog sat down stiffly at the table in a corner with a large square bush protecting his back. Karma plopped down at his feet and stretched out. Well, at least one of them looked comfortable.

"You can call me Darwin, you know. 'Ma'am' makes me feel like my mother."

"Sorry." He nodded. "Darwin it is."

"You're a trip, Mad Dog. All right, sit tight, I'll be right back." As I waited in line, breathing in raspberry and other exotic scents, I kept glancing back out the opened front door. I just figured he would bolt before I could feed them a hot meal. Why did I care? Looks like they've been doing fine on their own. Probably the same reason I snuck baby birds and abandoned kittens into the house, despite my mother's protests. I just did. Couldn't help it.

I spun around from checking the door and bam! A hot cup of tea was dripping down the front of my apron—which I had, to my embarrassment, forgotten to take off—and blazing a trail down my bare leg. "Ouch! Oh!" I glanced up at the man I had spun into. "Oh, oh, sorry!" Heavens, I really had to get used to other people standing in such close proximity to me.

Pursing his lips in an amused smile, he strolled to the counter, released a fist full of napkins from the holder and placed his cup on the counter. "Sandy, can I get another when you get a chance, please."

As he moved back toward me, the gold badge clipped to his belt glinted. I took in the white dress shirt, gray slacks, tie and neatly cropped hair and groaned. Perfect.

"Thanks." I hung my head as I accepted the napkins. "I'm really so sorry...officer?" I glanced up into his blue eyes as my hand brushed his. A small, electric charge zinged through me, bringing with it the smell of coconut and a weird feeling of euphoria. I jerked my hand away. *What was that?*

"Detective." He looked down on me from his 6'4ish vantage point.

My head buzzed like I'd had too much caffeine as I wiped at my apron with the napkins.

"Detective, right. Well," I straightened up and ignored the distracting scent and vibrations. "Let me buy you another tea, it's the least I can do."

He held my gaze and the tingling intensified until I had to rub my arms for relief.

"Detective Blake?" the girl at the counter called. "Got your refill."

He cleared his throat and broke our eye contact. "Some other time."

He nodded to her, grabbed his cup and left without another glance my way.

Some other time? What did that mean? Okay, weird.

"Next," the girl called.

***

"Here we go." I slid the tray on the table and placed a steaming ham and Swiss cheese omelet in front of Mad Dog with a cup of black tea, then a second one on the ground for Karma. "Should be able to gum some eggs," I said, as the drooling mastiff stuck his face in the dish. Entertainment at its finest.

"I can't pay you back." An uncomfortable, dark expression flashed across Mad Dog's face as he ripped open a raw sugar packet.

"You are paying me back by keeping me company." I stirred honey into my white tea, mala bead bracelets clacking on my wrist. "I'm the new girl in town, remember?"

"Sure. Thank you." Mad Dog nodded, slid an arm around the plate and moved a forkful of steaming omelet toward his mouth. "We appreciate your kindness."

I bit into a buttery croissant and eyed my breakfast company. "So, Mad Dog, what's your story?"

"My story?" he asked, around a mouthful of food.

"Yeah, everyone's got a story, right? What's yours?"

His weary eyes searched my face. The whole social aspect of human interaction, and how much butting in was polite, still baffled me. Maybe I had crossed the line?

Then he shrugged. "Persian Gulf and Iraq war vet turned homeless bum. Not much to tell." His slow, self effacing words were hard to swallow. Thick waves of despair washed over me.

I sipped my tea, forcing down the lump and waited for the emotional storm to subside.

After an uncomfortable minute, it did. "Well, that's not very nice."

His shoulder moved slightly and his expression stayed neutral. "The world ain't nice."

"The world is what you make it." At least that's what I've always believed. Of course, it was easy to believe that back home, in our controlled corner of the world. But what about here in this balmy, enchanting city with a history and trajectory of its own?

Mad Dog sat back, scrubbed his mouth with the paper napkin and studied me. "You grow up with money?"

I popped a few blueberries into my mouth and crunched, holding his gaze. "I suppose, yes." Though I never did like where that money came from. Or should I say *who* it came from?

"Then you were sheltered from the real world, Darwin."

I didn't want to admit it, but his words stung. Being sheltered was part of the reason I'd left home. I moved here to change that. And I liked hanging around Mad Dog because he didn't judge me. Was I wrong? I moved my gaze across Beach Avenue to the sun-dappled park. "Well, you could teach me about the real world then."

"I wouldn't wish what I know about the world on my worst enemy. Let alone a kind soul like you." He managed a small dry smile, though his eyes remained sad. "Thanks for the meal." He stacked our plates and stood. Karma pushed himself up, yawned and stretched.

"Sure," I said. "Same time tomorrow morning?"

Mad Dog eyed me with caution, lifting his back pack from the ground. "If you have something that needs done at the store. As long as it doesn't require staying indoors too long."

"Deal." I could find something for him to do. Not indoors though? Hmmm. Why ever not? Mind your own beeswax, Darwin. Not something I excelled at. "Okay. See you two in the morning. Bye, Karma." The dog swung his head around with a big, panting grin. I watched them cross the street then headed back to the boutique. Almost time to open up.

THREE

By Thursday I was exhausted but happy our first week open was going so well.

Just from walk-by traffic and word of mouth alone, Sylvia's grooming book filled up for the next three weeks, which she celebrated with a box of apple and lemon tarts. We also had a good idea of which products were going to be a hit in the area. These folks definitely liked to pamper their pets and we definitely enjoyed helping them do it.

I busied myself in the boutique straightening up and signaled "five minutes" to Mad Dog as he wiped down the glass double doors. It was the only thing I could come up with outside, but it made him comfortable enough to accept breakfast for his effort. We had grown into this easy routine. He would show up at seven, we would do the morning duties and then head over to Hooker Tea Company for breakfast before I opened up.

This morning, I got a small shock when I stepped out to greet them.

"Good heavens, Mad Dog, what happened to your face?" A bruise had formed a purple half-moon under his eye.

"This ain't no biggie, Darwin. Always trouble to be found when other people are involved." He leaned the squeegee handle against the front door. I noticed he was babying his right side, too.

"Well, did you file a police report, at least?"

He just shook his head and walked with a slight limp on our way to breakfast. I kept eyeing him sideways, my concern mounting as I thought about his situation. It must have been a big guy to get the jump on Mad Dog—or lots of guys. He and Karma made a formidable target. I remembered how quickly he had pinned me down on our first meeting. What kind of skill and strength would take to actually hurt him?

I carried out our usual omelets and slid into the chair under the umbrella. "So, you know, if you need a place to stay for a few days, you're welcome to my couch." I fiddled with the tea timer, hoping I wasn't crossing that line again. I didn't have much experience with people period, let alone people in Mad Dog's situation.

"I'm not really an indoor type guy, Darwin, and you shouldn't go around making offers like that to homeless guys. They can be dangerous. Could get yourself hurt." He dropped a croissant on Karma's dish. "You can't be so trusting."

I watched Karma sniff it then go back to his omelet. I waved him off. "You're harmless." Why was he homeless, though? He seemed perfectly capable of holding a job, mentally stable. Drug problem? Police record? Okay, I would just have to be nosey. "What does that mean, exactly, 'not an indoor guy' and where do you stay then?" I had assumed in a shelter. Don't cities have shelters for people with no place to go?

"Military shrinks call it PTSD. It just means screwed up." He shrugged in that self-depreciating way that made my heart ache. "I was involved in door to door urban battles so I prefer to be out in the open now. As far as where I stay, you don't know about Pirate City?"

Pirate City? Was he pulling my leg? Swallowing a mouthful of warm tea, I shook my head.

"Not part of the tourist attractions so I'm not surprised. Just a bunch of homeless people in tents, unmoored from society and trying to survive day to day."

Tents? I glanced at him to make sure he wasn't joking. "So what do y'all do for things like food and clothes?"

A dark cloud passed over his face. "Whatever we can."

I grew silent. Karma finished his breakfast, burped and rested his fifty pound head in my lap. I tensed up and waited. No image. No influx of energy. I usually only got zapped by animals who had suffered recent trauma—emotional or physical, big or small. Karma was a happy dog. I stroked his velvety ear.

Did Mad Dog mean illegal stuff? Is that why he wasn't willing to file a police report for getting beat up? Did he try to steal something and get caught? Guilt crept in. Why did I automatically jump to something illegal? Am I judging him because he's homeless? This interaction out in the world was so complicated. Just to clear my own conscience, I asked out loud, "So, nothing to do with drugs, right?"

"Naw. I managed to stay clear of that nightmare. I'm one of the lucky ones. Been sober for five months, too. Being responsible for another soul has been a life-saver. Ain't that right, Karma?" Mad Dog shook his head at Karma, who cocked an eyebrow his way but didn't move his head from my lap. "I think someone has a crush." He drained his cup and reached down for the licked-clean plate.

"I think someone just appreciates a good meal," I laughed, scratching under his ear with one hand and wiping at the drool on my leg with the other. Too bad scientists haven't come up with something useful for dog drool, like spackling houses.

"Speakin' of..." Mad Dog pulled a twenty dollar bill from his pocket and shoved it under my empty plate. "This one's on me today." I started to protest but he stood up. "I insist. Come on, Karma. Time to go, boy."

"All right." I frowned. "I guess I should say thank you, then. See y'all tomorrow." Karma huffed after Mad Dog as he crossed the street. I picked up the twenty and sighed. He should have used it on something he needed. Well, I'd just buy some supplies for Karma and give them to him tomorrow. I considered his injuries as I walked back to the boutique. Maybe I should buy him some aspirin, too.

FOUR

We were in the last hour of a busy day when Sylvia strolled up to greet a new customer.

"*Aí what precioso bebês!*" She plucked a tiny long coated Chihuahua from the girl's pink croc doggie purse. Another one popped her head up. Soon other customers had surrounded them, ooooing and ahhhhing over the puppies. "What you need for these babies?" Sylvia asked, cuddling one under her chin and stroking the one huddled in the purse.

The girl flicked a curly, auburn lock off her shoulder. "Well, my boss, Frankie Maslow, these are her new puppies, and she heard about the flower essence therapy you have here. She wanted me to get something that would help them adjust to their new home. Little buggers whine all night."

"Ah, Frankie. Okay. This, you would need Darwin for. Darwin!" Sylvia called.

"Yes?" I stepped out from behind the counter, where I had been watching the exchange while opening a fresh shipment of botanical shampoos and flushable poop bags. "Cute babies! What can I help you with?"

"*Eu sei*, couldn't you just eat them up?" Sylvia kissed the one in her hand on her glistening nose and placed the pup reluctantly back in the purse. "This lady needs something for her boss's pups to help calm the *bebês*, help them adjust to their new home and sleep at night."

"Sure, no problem." I eyed her leather mini skirt and biker boots. "Why don't you have a look around, see if there's anything else you need while I get that for you."

On my way to the back, I plucked a bottle of fish oil from the top shelf for an elderly lady cradling a plump poodle who was about to bring the whole shelf down on herself. Mental note: People shrink with age, and St. Pete did used to be known as "God's waiting room." I needed to lower the shelves.

"Here we go. Honeysuckle, Mariposa Lily and Cosmos." I showed the girl the bottles before wrapping them in tissue, timing my words between her gum snaps. "Four drops a few times a day, massage into the pups' skin. Should have them sleeping like babies by the end of the week. I'll put a discount card in your bag. When they're ready for a grooming, Sylvia will be happy to take care of them."

"Sure. I'll take these, too." She dropped some organic chews on the counter along with two tiny, glow-in-the-dark t-shirts.

"Those are fabulous!" Sylvia swooned. "Please tell Frankie Sylvia Alvarez said 'hi'."

"Will do, thanks." After one last cuddle from Sylvia, the pups disappeared out the door.

"Charming girl. You know her boss?" I asked.

"Everyone knows her." Sylvia moved closer and lowered her voice. "Frankie Maslow was homeless then she won the lottery four years ago. Thirty million, I think. *Afortunado!* Took a lump sum of seventeen million. Now she look down on St. Pete from the Vinoy. But," she held up a finger. "She has not forgotten. Every Sunday morning, she go to Mirror Lake and hand out hot meals to the homeless. She has a good heart but some, they try to stop what she is doing. They say she is encouraging them to sleep downtown and residents are *apreensivo*... afraid of them."

"Sounds complicated." I'd like to meet this woman. Maybe we could pair up and do a charity dog wash or something to raise money for the homeless. Ever since I'd met Mad Dog, I'd been brainstorming for ways to help.

***

Friday had finally arrived. I watched Mad Dog limp across Beach Drive and frowned. The chores could wait. I stepped out into the morning sunshine, locked the doors behind me and crossed my arms. Karma spotted me and lumbered in my direction, his large rump and tail wagging slowly.

"Good Mornin'."

"Don't you good morning me, Mad Dog." I shook my head at the purple knot on his right cheek bone. I had watched all week as he arrived with fresh injuries and I'd had enough. "I'm taking you to the police station and you are going to report whoever is doing this to you."

"Can't do that," he sighed. "It's my own fault."

"I don't understand."

He dropped his head. "Maybe I shouldn't come around anymore. I don't want to upset you."

"What? No!" My chest squeezed at the thought. "All right. I'll stop asking you to go to the police if you promise that you'll think about telling me what's going on with you. It's just hard seeing you like this every day."

"I'll think about it."

I glanced down at Karma. He didn't look very happy either. "All right. Let's go get breakfast."

When we were situated with our food at the table, Mad Dog turned to me. "So, what's your story?"

"My story?" I plopped my chin down on my hand.

"Yeah, everyone's got one, right?" He brushed an ant off the table.

I raised an eyebrow as he gave me a rare smile. "Are you teasing me?"

"No, I really want to know."

I stirred my tea and shrugged. "All right, what do you want to know?"

He watched a group of bicyclists navigate Beach Drive and then turned back to me. "Well, for starters, how'd you get a name like Darwin?"

"Oh, going right for the jugular, huh?" I grinned. "Well, if you really want to know, my mom got knocked up with me at seventeen and named me Darwin to be spiteful to her overbearing, religious parents."

He stopped chewing and stared at me. "Seriously?"

"Yep."

A laugh escaped him that startled Karma. "That's great. I think I'd like your mom."

I hadn't ever heard him laugh before. It was nice. "Glad I could be your entertainment this morning."

"Where's your family? Carolinas?"

"My mother was raised there, yeah. But I grew up in Savannah. The southern twang gave me away, right?"

He nodded. "So, what brought you to St. Pete?"

"Sylvia." I chewed and swallowed a bite of omelet. "We met on a bulletin board. We were both attending an online business school. Just hit it off and kept in touch. When she had an idea for a pet boutique, she ran it by me. I had the money to invest in it with her and so, here we are."

"And your family was okay with you leaving?"

"You mean escaping?" I frowned. "No. But, I'm hoping they'll forgive me eventually." I downed the last of my tea and wiped at the sweat trickling down my bare neck. I may have to switch to iced tea tomorrow. "So, what about you? Your family from here?"

A haunted look gripped him, like he had just remembered something terrible. "My parents are gone. No siblings." He reached down and picked up Karma's empty plate. Karma took this as his cue and grunted as he pushed himself off the ground and stretched.

Oh, I forgot. "Hey, Mad Dog? You know Frankie Maslow?"

"Mama Maslow? Yeah, sure. Good lady. Millionaire and still takes time out to feed people. Why?"

"Oh, I met her assistant yesterday. She brought in Frankie's new puppies. I was thinking about asking if she wanted to team up for a fund raiser for the homeless. Is that something you think she'd be interested in?"

Mad Dog rubbed his buzzed scalp and stood. "Sure, I guess. Just stay clear of her boyfriend, Vick. Guy's bad news."

"Thanks for the tip." I watched him shrug a shoulder into his backpack. "Hey, you be careful." He waved without turning back. I did realize how ridiculous it sounded. Me telling this military trained tough guy to be careful, but I really was worried. What's going on with all the injuries? And why were they his fault? I had to find some way to make him open up.

FIVE

I rose with the morning sun and decided on a bike ride to Mirror Lake to see if I could talk to Frankie Maslow. I missed my sisters more on Sundays. Sundays back home had been something we always looked forward to. No work, just pancakes and gardening and girl talk. Neither one of my sisters were speaking to me right now, though. They couldn't understand why I needed to leave, why I wanted to leave. Being "different" had never been a problem for them. I, on the other hand, wanted a normal life surrounded by people who considered me to be normal. I could only hope that one day they would understand.

It was another gorgeous June morning, filled with the sounds of light traffic and bird songs. The sky was a soft metallic silver, brushed with wispy gray clouds as I steered onto the Third Avenue sidewalk. A few early risers perused the area. The ride to Mirror Lake should only take fifteen minutes but I had packed an iced water bottle, a bagel and some fruit in case I had to wait for Frankie to show up.

As I approached the road that circled around Mirror Lake, a ferocious barking echoed off the surrounding buildings from the other side. My muscles tensed. Could I outrun an angry dog on a bike? I hoped so. I steered off Mirror Lake Dr. and onto the sidewalk, my curiosity piqued as the barking grew more insistent.

As I rounded the final bend, I could see police cars in the gated parking lot and a crowd of people in the grass. When I pulled around behind the police cars, I dropped my bike and weaved my way through the crowd. What was going on? Two of the officers had their guns drawn and pointed at the lake. A few others were trying to get the spectators to back up. I wasn't real comfortable around guns but I was even less comfortable with an animal in distress.

I slipped deeper into the crowd as another round of ferocious barking began. What had the poor thing so riled up? "Excuse me," I said, feeling my foot come down on someone else's. "Sorry."

Then I froze as I emerged in front of the crowd and could see down the slight embankment. My heart almost stopped. A body lay sprawled out, face down in the grass near the lip of the water. And there, standing over it was Karma.

"Karma!" I cried. Then I ran. Yep, under the police tape, straight to the place where the guns were pointed. Not my brightest moment, I know. But, I'd read enough stories to realize Karma was in danger of being shot. He was big and barking like a slathering, crazed beast. The police were probably scared of him but needed to get to the man.

I heard someone yell, "Stop!" from a distance, but I kept focused on Karma, who was now turned my way, his ears up, eyes alert. My sandals slipped in the wet grass and I fell hard on my knees in front of Karma. I looked up. "It's okay, boy. It's okay." He was hot and panting. He collapsed beside the man and laid his head on the man's back with a whimper.

"Mad Dog!"

"Ma'am, step away!" Two officers had followed and now had guns pointed at me. "You can't be here!"

"Stop pointing guns at us and help my friend!" I pointed at Mad Dog. "Please!" They were staring at Karma with skeptical fear.

"Oh for heaven's sakes, he's not gonna bite y'all. He doesn't even have any teeth!" My southern twang really emerged in a crisis.

At that moment, a man in a suit pushed between the officers and told them to lower their weapons. It took my panicked brain a few seconds to realize I knew this man. The detective I had spilled tea on. Perfect. He came forward with a nylon rope and held it out to me. His eyes met mine and sparked with recognition.

"Ma'am, I'm Detective Blake. You seem to know this dog, if you would lead him away from the victim so we can do our job, I'd appreciate it."

Oh, thank heavens. I took the rope and looped it around Karma's thick neck. As I did, he licked the side of my head with a dry tongue. Zap!

***

I fell back, landing in the water. As the vision-energy lit up my brain like the Fourth of July, a sequence of shots played in fast forward. A townhouse. Running down streets. Water splashing as I jumped in the lake, Mad Dog's body floating. The images came with red hot rage and searing white sadness. I cried out as my skin burned from the inside out.

Detective Blake was leaning down, talking to me but I couldn't hear anything beyond the rush of energy like the ocean in my own head. The lake water began to churn around me. I forced myself up and tried to jog in place. Dizziness threatened to knock me back on my butt. This was bad. Real, real bad.

Once in awhile, an animal's trauma would hurt slightly, sort of like a jolt of electricity, but this felt like a nuclear explosion. A lake breeze blew over my wet shorts and sweaty face but the heat was still building, scalding me from the inside out.

"I have to go for a quick run," I heard myself say from inside a tunnel. That sounded rational, right? I tried for some jumping jacks.

"Are you all right?" Detective Blake tried to catch my eye as I bounced up and down. I shook my head. I have to run! But it was too late.

Pop! Pop! Pop!

The officers surrounding me spun around and drew their weapons at the series of loud pops. A collective gasp came from the crowd. I didn't have to look. I had blown out lights before. This time the victims were the police cruiser headlights.

I did feel better though. The chaos in my body began to subside. I stopped jumping up and down like a crazy person and rested my palms on my knees, doubled over, breathing hard.

"Seriously, are you okay? We have a medic on site."

I waved him off. "Hot flashes. I'm okay now." I wrapped my arms around Karma and replayed each image, burning them into my memory. "Okay, boy. I saw. I saw and we're going to figure it out together."

"What the hell?" The tall officer walked over to join the others as they inspected the cars.

Time to skedaddle before the questions started. "Come on, boy." He resisted, looking from me to Mad Dog. "Come on, Karma. Let the nice men do their job." I wiped at the sweat dripping down my chin and the tears blurring my vision. I couldn't bring myself to look back at Mad Dog. I knew he was gone. I had to concentrate on helping Karma now.

"All right, Ma'am. Please wait by the police cars. We'll need to speak with you." Detective Blake waved the team of people over that were standing by.

I grabbed his big head and made him focus on me. "You have to come with me now, Karma. He's gone." With one last whine, Karma stood up—his head and tail hanging—and walked away from his best friend. His body pressed against mine as we trudged back up the embankment and under the police tape. I was numb and my legs felt like jelly. I whispered to Karma, trying to sooth him. I led him to my bike and grabbed the ice water before walking back over to wait by the police cars but he wouldn't drink it.

We sat in the grass, my arm draped across Karma, stroking his bristly fur. I watched as officers took pictures, put things in bags and eventually brought over a large white bag to zip Mad Dog up into. I noticed Karma lift his head at this point, his brow furrowed deep between alert brown eyes and he softly whimpered.

"I'm sorry, boy." I let the tears fall and said a few silent words for Mad Dog.

SIX

The crowd had begun to disperse. Detective Blake smelled like suntan lotion and fresh air as he squatted beside me with a notepad. I stared up into his face, which was all I could do at this point. I was drained and going into emotional shock. Karma was my lifeline and I was holding onto him tight.

"You doing all right? Looked like you were going to pass out there for a minute."

"Been better." I forced a smile because he really did look concerned. It didn't work, though. He was still frowning at me.

"So...Miss?"

"Winters. Darwin Winters."

He scribbled in his notebook. "I assume you knew the victim?"

"Yes. He was my friend. Mad Dog." Then it occurred to me I didn't even know his real name. This threatened to burst through the numbness with a bucket load of tears. I choked them back. "I... guess that wasn't his real name."

"It's all right. We can ID him through fingerprints. Probably has a record."

"Why do you say that? He was a nice guy."

"He was homeless. They usually have been arrested for something...loitering, theft, public intoxication. Can I get an address and phone number?"

I was busy biting my tongue.

"Ma'am?" He held up the pen expectantly, his eyes darting over my face.

"Of course." I gave him the information. "You know, he was a Gulf War Veteran. He fought for our country and that's why he was homeless. He wasn't lazy or a drug addict. He had PS...TD..." I stopped. Was that right? PTDS?

"Post traumatic stress disorder." Detective Blake's mouth bent into a slight, curious smile. "How long did you know him?"

"We had breakfast every morning together this week." Saying it out loud, it didn't seem so long. "Long enough for me to know he had found some kind of trouble. Do you think you'll be able to catch who did this?"

I should have known when he took too long to answer me.

"This will probably be ruled a suicide."

"What?" I sat up straighter and felt Karma tense up beside me and focus on the detective. "No! He wouldn't take his own life. He wouldn't leave Karma." I motioned to the mastiff.

He turned his head and looked back at the lake, weighing something. "There was an empty bottle of Bacardi 8 Rum a few feet away."

I shook my head. "Well, that doesn't mean he drank it. He had been sober for five months."

"It's a rough existence, Miss Winters. People with easier lives fall off the wagon every day. Trust me. I've seen it too many times. He probably got intoxicated and drowned. On purpose or not."

I couldn't believe it. I glanced down at Karma. The images I picked up from him were not of a suicide. But how could I explain it? I couldn't just say, '*Hey, I got these psychic images from the dog so I know something else happened here.*' He wouldn't believe me anyway. And it would definitely end my quest to be considered normal. I sighed. Then remembered something I *could* say.

"He'd been showing up every day with new bruises and pretty beat up. Don't you think it's odd that he would end up..." I couldn't say it out loud. "You know, after someone had obviously been violent with him?"

"There's always violence in Pirate City. An autopsy will be performed, though, so if you want to check with me in a month or so, the report should be filed and I can let you know for sure." He dug out a card and held it out. "Thank you for your time." Then he glanced down at Karma. "Are you willing to take responsibility for his dog?"

"Yes, of course." And then something occurred to me. "Wait. If he doesn't have any family, how will there be a funeral?"

"If we can't locate next of kin, he'll be cremated and his remains will be scattered in the Gulf eventually."

I suddenly felt like I was going to throw up. "Thank you." I clutched his card in one hand and pushed myself off of the ground with the other. "Come on, Karma. Let's go home."

SEVEN

"You look like death!" Monday morning, Sylvia arrived, locked the boutique door behind her and hurried over to me. She, on the other hand, looked like an angel in her white linen pant suit, her liquid eyes full of concern. "What's going on?" She paused, the wad of keys dangling off her finger. "And who is this?"

"Sylvia meet Karma... Karma, this is Sylvia." I heard the listlessness in my voice, but I couldn't find the energy to care. Karma shared my bed last night because he wouldn't leave my side and he snored. Loud. All night. Besides being sad, I was exhausted.

"*Alô*, Karma." Her hands rested on her hips. "This is the homeless guy's dog, no?"

"Yes. Mad Dog is... gone." I pulled myself up off the stool. "The police think it was a suicide, but it wasn't."

Sylvia stood, staring from me to Karma, processing this. Finally, a string of Portuguese came out on a long sigh. I have no idea what she said, but I knew she had grasped the situation.

"Okay. Karma, you smell bad. If you're going to stay here, you need a bath." She dropped her keys in the drawer beneath the counter and clapped her hands. Karma lifted his head. "Come on, *pobre cão*. Let's get you cleaned up so you don't run our customers out of here."

To my surprise, Karma pushed himself up and lumbered after her. I watched him go, his head and tail still hanging. I felt the stirrings of dark emotions. Anger, for one. I replayed the images I had received from Karma. There was a townhouse, gray with an A frame in front, flat roof in back; then Karma ran down a street, then jumped in the water, swimming. He must have pulled Mad Dog from the water. How did Mad Dog get in the water? Karma always stayed by Mad Dog's side. So, why was Karma running down the street alone?

I picked Detective Blake's card up from the counter and stared at it. Should I just tell him what I saw? Would he even believe me? Probably not. No, I had to find real evidence. Something to make him investigate Mad Dog's death as a...a what? A murder? My heart jumped. Well, if it wasn't a suicide then that's what it was, right? Murder.

Oh, Mad Dog...what did you get yourself into? I didn't know, but I was going to find out.

Karma turned out to be a big hit with our customers. He spent the day sprawled out by the counter, his head on his paws, sad brown eyes watching the comings and goings from beneath a wrinkled brow. Sylvia had scrubbed him until his fur shined and fixed a new baby blue collar around his neck. I rubbed blackberry and honeysuckle essence into his skin a few times that day, hoping to ease his grief. He turned down food and I had to spritz water on his tongue to get some fluid into him.

Being busy helped but by the end of the day, when we locked the doors and flipped the closed sign around, the sadness crept back and settled over me like a heavy blanket.

Sylvia came over and lifted my chin in her hand. "Come on, let's get some dinner and you can tell me what happened to your friend."

We ended up at Parkshore Grill's patio style tables on the corner, a pet friendly restaurant so Karma wouldn't be left alone. Sylvia had a fondness for the place, since it was one of the first restaurants to take a chance on Beach Drive a few years ago and start the upswing into the successful tourist destination it was now.

I ordered Karma an unseasoned steak, which I cut into tiny pieces, and a bowl of ice water. Both of which, he stared at with disinterest. I rubbed his ears. I kept hoping to get more images from him, a clearer picture of the events but got nothing.

"So, spill the beans, *my amiga.*" Sylvia poured from the bottle of Jadot Burgundy she ordered for us to split. "Such a tragedy. How did this happen?"

"I honestly don't know. I went to Mirror Lake early yesterday morning, hoping to meet Frankie and talk to her about doing a fundraiser for the homeless. But, when I got there, the police were there with their guns pointed at Karma, who was just having a fit protecting Mad Dog." My insides trembled. The scene was still too fresh. I took a mouthful of wine, letting it calm my insides before I continued. "When I realized Mad Dog was... dead..." there, I said it. Dead. Gone forever. Oh heavens, the last time I saw him...was the last time I would ever see him. My eyes blurred, my heart felt raw. I looked up at Sylvia, using her as an anchor. "I didn't even know his real name."

She placed a dry hand over mine on the table. "We can find out his real name, then we can say a prayer for his soul." She glanced down at Karma. "We'll say a prayer for you, too, *pobre bebê.*" She pushed the coconut shrimp appetizer around on her plate. I could see her looking at me sideways. "You don't believe he took his own life?"

"No."

She sighed. "Well, that's a good thing for his soul."

"I think someone murdered him."

"Why you think this?" She glanced around nervously.

What could I say? If flower essence was on her woo-woo list, me receiving psychic images from Karma would really freak her out. "Um, well, the detective told me there was an empty bottle of rum..." I reached into my memory, "Bacardi 8, found near the body. So they think he got intoxicated and drowned."

"Whoa, expensive bottle of rum for a homeless guy."

"But that's just it; he'd been sober for five months. He said because of Karma. He would have never willingly left him." Her words just hit me. "Expensive? Like how expensive?"

She shrugged. "Around a thousand dollars American."

"Huh." Well, that didn't make sense. At all. "Well, I don't think it was his anyway. The detective said they'll be able to tell when they do a tox screen during the autopsy." A month, though or more. Jeez. Whoever murdered him could be long gone by then. I had to find a way to get them to investigate this as a murder before then.

"I have to figure out what happened to him."

Sylvia waved her fork at me, swallowing in a hurry. "No, no, no you don't. If he was killed by someone, you can't go putting yourself in danger by trying to expose the killer. Don't you watch crime shows?"

I shrugged. "Actually, no." We never had a TV in our house. I did read a lot, but that would only give Sylvia ammunition for her argument, so I kept that to myself. "Sylvia, Mad Dog was my friend. I have to do something."

"That's what the police are for. Us civilian folk, we say prayers."

I just nodded and took a bite of salad. We would just have to disagree on this point. Karma huffed and moved to rest against my foot. I reached down and stroked his head. Yeah, I know, boy. Don't worry. We're not letting Mad Dog's killer get away with it. But, what could I do to get Detective Blake to investigate now? I could ask him about the price of the rum. Where would

Mad Dog get money for that? Wasn't that suspicious enough? That along with all his recent injuries should account for something.

I dug into my meal with new determination. I would call the detective first thing in the morning.

EIGHT

Tuesday morning brought me right back to square one. Detective Blake knew about the price of the rum. Apparently a few homeless guys had robbed a liquor store a few weeks before Mad Dog's death, so they were chalking it up to that. That only left me with trying to figure out how he was getting hurt. I ended the conversation by reiterating the fact that he didn't drink. Weak, yeah, but the best I could do, for now.

After we closed up shop for the day, I clipped a lead on Karma and walked him to the Seventh Avenue dog park. The leash was purely for show. If he really wanted to go somewhere, my little willowy 5'8, 120 pound frame wasn't going to stop him. It was still about ninety degrees out, so by the time we got there, sweat rolled down my face and sides and Karma was panting like a freight train. I poured a trickle of bottled water in front of his mouth and he reached out and lapped at it until strings of foamy drool hung from his jowls. A good sign. Maybe I could get him to eat something tonight.

I closed the gate behind us and unclipped the lead. There were quite a few dogs there. Two retrievers with shiny gold coats pranced up to sniff him. I waved to the elegant looking woman who had been tossing them a tennis ball.

"Hello, pretty girls," I said, stroking the silky fur. "Karma, do you want to play?" They lost interest when he just stood there with his head hanging and romped off after a squirrel.

I had hoped being around his own kind would snap Karma out of his funk but it didn't look like a successful ploy. He lumbered over to a semi-shaded area beneath a large palm and flopped down on the ground, his head between his paws. With a sigh, I followed and plopped down on the bench beside him. So much for that theory.

"Oh, Karma," I rubbed his ear between my fingers. "I know you're sad. But Mad Dog wouldn't have wanted to see you like this. You have to snap out of this, boy."

A black German shepherd came over to investigate us. He sniffed the air in front of Karma without approaching him.

"Gorgeous mastiff. What's his name?"

I looked up at the man who had come around the tree to stand beside the German shepherd. Wow, whoever said people look like their dogs really had some insight. This guy was lean and dark, wearing a black t-shirt and dark Ray Bans.

"Thanks, his name's Karma. He lost his owner a few days ago, so I'm trying to get him out of a funk." I motioned to the black shepherd, who had sat down beside his master, keeping an alert eye on us. He looked pretty intimidating with those stark white canines and gold eyes. Of course, his owner was a shoe in for Mr. Dark and Mysterious of the year. "How about yours?"

"I call him Mage. His registered name is Black Magick."

Nice accent. British, maybe? "Nice to meet you, Mage." I reached up to shake his hand.

"I'm Darwin."

"Landon Stark, pleased to meet you."

Something about Mr. Stark felt familiar and not in a good way. "Likewise."

"Vacationing?"

"No. I came here to open up a pet boutique with a friend, Darwin's on Beach Drive?"

"Ah, yes. The place is getting quite a good reputation around here. Congratulations."

"Thanks. My partner, Sylvia, and I are very happy with the response so far."

"Wow, that's great. And it's not even season. I'll have to stop in and see what all the fuss is about." He smiled and I tried to figure out if I knew him from somewhere. Had I seen him around town? "Well, good luck getting your friend there to cheer up."

"Thanks." I waved goodbye and then glanced down at Karma. "What do ya think, boy? Friend or foe?" He cut his eyes sideways at me. "Okay, I get it. This isn't your cup of tea. Let's head back."

He plodded along beside me, his toenails clicking on the warm concrete when we had to use the sidewalk. I tried to keep him in the grass as much as possible in case the cement was too hot on his pads. What else would cheer up a grieving dog? Food and belly rubs was all I could think of and those weren't working. Neither, it seemed, was the flower essence. Maybe he just needed time. Or…

I stopped in the middle of the sidewalk and Karma looked up at me, ears perched in a questioning pose. Maybe there was someone else in Mad Dog's life that Karma would respond to. Maybe a friend at…what did he call the place? Pirate City? Yeah, that's it!

"Want to go visit Pirate City, boy?" His gaze kept locked on mine. "I'll take that as a yes." I led him forward again. Now I just had to find out where it was. Oh, and bonus, maybe someone there knew something about how Mad Dog was getting those injuries. I don't know why I didn't think of this sooner.

NINE

I couldn't just ask Sylvia about Pirate City because she would start yelling at me in Portuguese for sure. I was learning quickly that her motto was 'mind your own business,' except when it came to me. She had become very protective of me, like a big sister. Not that I minded, considering how much I missed my own sisters. It was easy enough to find on the internet though. Lots of local news articles. Apparently having a homeless tent city in the area was quite the sore spot to a lot of folks. I made a plan to take Karma there on Saturday morning.

"Karma, we're going to go visit your old stomping ground, boy." I plopped down beside him on the polished teak floor, ignored the dust bunnies and stared out the French doors. Night had fallen. The lantern-style porch light illuminated my flower garden and—beyond the black iron railing—tiny white lights twinkled in the park trees. Beyond those, the moon lit up the bay waters. Karma repositioned his head to fill my lap.

"The treats are almost done. You're not going to be able to resist the peanut butter ones, I'm telling you now." I kissed the wrinkles on his wide head, between his ears, then rested my forehead on the space and slowed my breathing, trying to open myself up to any images he might send me. Anything else you remember about that night? Anything at all that would help me find out what really happened?

I had never wanted to have control over this gift before. I just took it as it came, used it when it happened to help whatever distressed animal I found. Even shunned it because I just wanted to be like everyone else. But, what I wouldn't give to be able to see more, to know what Karma knew about that night. The oven dinged. One more kiss and I pushed myself off the floor.

I pulled the treats from the oven, filling the place with the smell of warm peanut butter. I had already made the chicken jerky for the boutique, but I didn't think Karma would be able to gum those. He'd probably end up swallowing it whole... if he was interested at all. I had tried plain chicken in broth when we got home. He lapped at the broth a bit, then assumed his position in front of the French doors and hadn't moved since. Was he watching for Mad Dog? Was he remembering their afternoons in the park? How much did pets understand? I wish I knew. His depression did seem to indicate that he at least missed Mad Dog greatly.

I wrapped cellophane around the treats and flipped off the lights. "Come on, Karma. Bedtime."

He navigated around the furniture, knocking my candles off the coffee table with his tail, followed me up the stairs and launched himself onto the bed. It creaked and moaned beneath his weight. "Hey, that's my side." I slipped out of my clothes and into a worn-thin cotton t-shirt, shaking my head. Actually it was both sides. "I've got some tricks up my sleeve, too, big guy." I pulled ear plugs out of the nightstand drawer, scratched his belly and pushed my way into bed. "Snore away, Karma. Sweet dreams."

TEN

"Okay, Karma, today's the big day." I unzipped my backpack and stuffed in bottles of water, organic raisin cookies, ten cans of Off bug spray, five packages of new t-shirts and a few packs of playing cards. A peace offering I hoped. Maybe it would help them trust me, to see that I only had Mad Dog's—and their—best interest at heart. I slipped into the back pack, threw on my straw hat and rubbed Karma's ears. "We're off."

It was a pretty good trek north, down a dead end street and into the woods. Karma jogged beside my bike the whole time, sitting to pant when I stopped to give us water and spray myself with bug spray. When we got to the edge of the woods, his demeanor shifted. His head and ears were now up. He seemed alert. It was a nice change from his moping. He took the lead down the well worn sandy path. I decided to walk my bike. Florida woods were different than Georgia woods. More leafless pine trees and overgrown palmetto bushes with loud bugs and frogs and things sent scurrying by our movement through their world.

"Ptt!" I spit. Bug. Flew. In. My. Mouth. "Ew!" I waved a hand in front of my face to discourage any more of his friends from trying it. Karma stopped and glanced back at me. I stared up at the sign above him, strung between two trees. The black and orange quintessential "NO TRESPASSING" sign along with a homemade "Pirate City- Keep Out!" Warning.

"Well, that's not exactly a welcome mat now is it, boy?" I leaned my bike against the tree and readjusted the back pack, which I had to say was heavy and I'd be glad to unload the goodies for more than one reason. "Lead the way, Karma."

He lumbered into the camp like a lion, his head still raised and alert, me behind him trying to get the moss off which had attached itself to my hat. When I looked up, I stopped to survey the camp.

It was a bit shocking. I mean, this wasn't like a camp where families roast marshmallows and teach their kids how to fish. This was a community in the rawest, most heartbreaking sense. Flimsy octagons of material and strung up blue tarps that people called home? How? How in this soaring Florida heat, summer storms and blood thirsty bugs did these people survive? It was mind boggling. Also, coming from the sprawling home that I did, I felt more than a twinge of guilt.

Karma was on the move again so I followed him through the dirty sand-mulch mixture right into the heart of the camp. There, I encountered a group of men who were standing around a makeshift table of plywood and stacked milk crates. I briefly thought about Mad Dog telling me the homeless could be dangerous, but these guys—by their wide eyes and startled glances—seemed more scared of me.

"Hello," I called out with a wave, moving toward them. "My name's Darwin. I was a friend of Mad Dog's." When I got within ten feet of them I stopped. The smell was bad. A mixture of body odor and hot garbage. Well, what did I expect? Not exactly any showers or trash pickup out here. Karma pressed against my leg so I rested a hand on his back. "Y'all remember Karma? Thought I'd bring him by for a visit. See some familiar faces. He's been in such a funk since Mad Dog left us."

A burst of laughter broke the silence and two of the men stepped forward. The younger one—with dirty blonde hair in a dreadlocked nest—crossed his arms and looked me up and down. I couldn't help but think of a pirate. Hence the name Pirate City, maybe?

"Well, this is a first, ain't it, Pops? Don't think we've ever had a visitor before."

"Not one we'd want anyhow." The large, Santa Clause looking guy chuckled. "Hey, Karma."

Karma sat down, relaxing, his tongue hanging down the side of his jowl. His eyes were still alert though.

The others started gathering in front of us.

"So, it's true then? What they said about Mad Dog? That he got hooched up and drowned?"

I tucked my hands into the pockets of my khaki shorts and shrugged. "That's what the police think."

"Pshh... po-po don't know nothing. Don't care to know about nothing." This came from a woman I hadn't noticed. She now pushed her way through to stand beside Pops.

"Mind your mouth, Minnie." A gray-haired man stepped out of a tent to our right. His skin was ruddy red and he wore only a pair of cut off jeans and flip flops. He looked at me suspiciously and then gave Karma a pat on the head. "Hey, Karma. We wondered where you'd gone off to. Got a new friend?"

"Darwin." I offered him my hand and he shook it roughly.

"Mac."

"Nice to meet you, Mac." Now would probably be a good time for my peace offering. I brought my backpack around to my front and unzipped it. "Mad Dog was a friend of mine. He told me about y'all and so I thought I'd bring some things that might be useful." I pulled out a t-shirt pack and held it out to the gathered crowd. No one moved forward. "No one?" Finally, the woman called Minnie reached out and took it with a soft "thanks." I noticed Mac watching me closely as I passed out the rest of the contents of the backpack. I also noticed that Karma had wandered off. When my back pack was emptied, I walked around the crowd and found Karma sniffing at a red and white tent.

"Whatcha doing, boy?"

"That there was Mad Dog's." Mac walked up behind me. I was beginning to guess he was sort of in charge of things in the camp. Probably the guy I needed to ask questions of then.

"You knew Mad Dog pretty well?"

"Well, it's not like we sit down and have heart to hearts in here or nothing." He crossed his arms and pushed his tongue into the side of his mouth, his eyes narrowing as he looked at me. "What'd you want with Mad Dog, anyhow?"

"I told you. He was my friend."

"Hm." He stared at me for a long while. I just waited. He seemed to push his suspicion aside. "So, you're not lookin' for his money?"

"Money?" Was this guy kidding? Or maybe he wasn't playing with a full deck? "No, sir. Why would I think Mad Dog had money?" That did bring back the memory of him laying the twenty down for breakfast. Did he have money? And if he did have money, did he buy the bottle of expensive rum? As I pondered this, Mac nodded.

"Well, I can tell you, I knew him well enough to know he wasn't drinkin'."

It was my turn to study him. I decided I believed him. Or at least I believed he believed he was telling the truth. That still didn't mean Mad Dog didn't fall off the wagon. Something had been going on with him. Maybe it had all got too much.

"Did you happen to know his real name?"

"Naw." Mac pursed his lips. "Can't say I could tell you anyone's real name here."

"Well, did he leave anything behind that might help me find his next of kin?"

"We have a plywood wall nailed to a couple a trees over there," he motioned behind me. "The folks who have family to speak of, someone they want to be told when they're gone, they write the information there. But Mad Dog, he never wrote on the wall."

"Oh." I watched Karma nose his way into the tent and then reappear a few moments later.

"He had a back pack that he carried with him but it wasn't at the lake when they found him. Did he leave it here?"

Mac thought for a moment and then called over my shoulder. "Hey, G!" He waved his arm. "Come here for a sec!" He leaned over to me. "G inherited Mad Dog's tent when he left us. Course, some of the others may have gotten into his stuff already. Hard to say."

G wandered over with a toothless grin, holding a half-eaten raisin cookie. His skin looked more like a brown leather mask, so it was hard to guess his age. My heart lurched a little at his apparent happiness with the cookie. Such a simple thing.

"Hello, G." I waved.

"Hey, G… you see Mad Dog's back pack anywhere? Was it in the tent?"

"Mad Dog's gone. Sad." His dark eyes were swollen and clouded by a milky film. Still, even though he was obviously mentally impaired, I could see the real emotion stirring.

"Yeah, it is sad, buddy." Mac put a hand on his shoulder, which helped him focus. "What about his back pack. You seen it?"

He lifted up his pant leg. "Socks. He left socks. And a flashlight. Oh yeah and a jacket. No back pack. Nope." His expression morphed from thoughtful to bright as he looked up at me. "Will you bring more cookies?"

"Sure, G. I can bring more cookies. Will you keep an eye out for Mad Dog's back pack for me?"

"Yes, nice lady." G wandered off then, munching as best he could on the rest of the cookie. His words warmed my insides. Then I spotted a man—well, teenager really—dark, greasy hair curling out from under a red bandana; olive skin; split, swollen lip and bandage over his right cheek.

"Hey, Mac. What happened to that kid over there?" Karma came and leaned against my leg. I rested a hand on his head.

Mac eyed the kid and then his gaze fell to the ground. "No offense, Miss, but this is a world you wouldn't understand. Violence is just part of that world." His sudden eye contact felt like a warning. I knew he wasn't going to offer anything more. I glanced back at the kid. Did Mad Dog and this kid get in a fight? Didn't seem likely. The kid was tall, but gangly. No match for Mad Dog. So, was someone else beating up the homeless? And did that have anything to do with Mad Dog's murder?

"Look," Mac said, resting his hands on his hips. "You're a nice girl. I suggest you go on about your life and forget about Mad Dog. Leave well enough alone."

Yeah, that was definitely a warning. Did he know something? I gave him my warmest smile and scratched Karma's head. "You're probably right. Mind if I just stop in once in awhile and bring Karma for a visit? This has seemed to perk him up. And, of course, I did promise G I'd bring more cookies."

He shook his head and shrugged, a gruff laugh escaping. "Guess there's a bit of crazy in everybody." He made a waving motion. "Do what you want. It's a free country."

"Thanks." I watched him disappear back into his tent. Bug spray hung thick in the air as I moved back through the knots of people. Karma walked behind me this time. "Bye, everyone." I kept my voice cheerful. "Bye, G!"

"Bye, nice lady." G grinned.

"See ya around, Snow White," one of the men called out. This was followed by a gaggle of laughter from the group. So, I had a nickname already, did I? I'd take that as a good sign.

I waved behind me as I crossed back under the 'No Trespassing' sign with my empty back pack slung over one shoulder.

ELEVEN

It started out as a quiet Monday morning. I was helping a gentleman with a red macaw perched on his shoulder and the bird kept repeating the sound of a computer booting up.

"I have a computer repair business," the man chuckled, scratching the bird affectionately under the chin. He apparently also had an unexpected litter of kittens with fleas and three iguanas in need of a larger cage.

"Busy household," I said, pulling some flea treatment and comb off the shelf. "We'll have to special order the larger cage. Come on," I was leading him to the counter when a woman entered the boutique with a bouncing mini greyhound puppy. We exchanged hellos and then she squealed as the puppy wiggled out of his collar and jumped up at the Macaw, gaining enough traction on the man's belt to almost reach him. The Macaw flapped his wings wildly but only managed to drop down on the glass counter.

"Lola! No, bad girl!" The woman scrambled to try and catch the thin charcoal gray pup, but the pup was having too much fun. She darted down the middle aisle and we could hear her slide into something with a crash. "I'm so sorry," the woman said, taking off after her. I exchanged a grin with the man as he placed the ruffled macaw back on his shoulder. Lola now ran up the aisle back toward us as her owner called her name over the noise of restacking the cans the pup had knocked down. Then Lola spotted Karma and bounced up to him, barking and jumping at his face, trying to get him to play. Karma lifted his head and watched the little tornado with fur for about ten seconds before he reached out his paw and pinned Lola to the wood floor. I rushed over and scooped up the puppy before her owner saw her baby beneath Karma's giant paw. "Good boy," I whispered to Karma, who huffed and dropped his head back on the bed.

Zap! I pulled Lola closer to my chest so I wouldn't drop her as the burst of energy shot through me. The abrupt alarm in my head made my insides tremble.

The woman appeared, out of breath, and took Lola from me, admonishing the little dog while I jogged over to the leash wall and did a few jumping jacks. Whew. Okay. I pulled a small pink harness with hand painted flowers off the wall and walked back over to Lola's owner.

"This will work much better for you than a collar." I slipped it on the puppy and tried to avoid wet kisses as I adjusted the harness to fit. "We've got a matching leash, too, if you'd like."

"Oh, sure. Thank you so much." I could hear the relief in her voice.

"Also," I tried to be matter of fact, "these dogs are very sensitive to noise. Fireworks, loud trucks," I caught her eye, "even alarm clocks."

We clipped the new leash on the harness and Lola bounced up and down. "Oh, really? Okay, thank you."

Sylvia heard the ruckus and came out to help. She rang the woman up while I ordered the man's iguana cage. The menagerie was leaving the store as another customer walked in.

"*Ah, Quem é esse homem?*"

"Hm?" I raised my head from the computer to glance at Sylvia. Not because I understood her question but because I understood her tone of appreciation. Something had caught her attention.

Turns out it was Mr. Dark and Mysterious from the dog park.

"Welcome to Darwin's Pet Boutique." Sylvia practically purred as he sauntered up to the counter, the black shepherd at his heels.

"Hello, Landon Stark, right?"

"Yes. Good afternoon, Darwin." He flashed me a wide smile and, sans sunglasses, his eyes were startling—black and shiny like a raven's. "And who do we have here?" He turned his intensity to Sylvia, and I thought I heard her breath catch in her throat as she offered him her hand.

"Sylvia Alvarez."

He lowered his mouth to her hand and brushed it with it lips. "Pleased to make your acquaintance, Sylvia Alvarez."

I did see the hair stand up on her arm then and fought to keep from rolling my eyes as she smiled, obviously completely under his spell. Did women really fall for this stuff? Was I just jealous because I'd never felt that kind of magic?

"Decided to come see what all the fuss was about, huh?" I crossed my arms. Why did I find him so suspicious?

"Yes. That and I wanted to give you some tickets to my show tonight." He reached into the pocket of his black silk shirt and pushed them across the counter.

I plucked one up. "Oh, you're a magician?" Well, that made sense—shady, secretive, twister of reality and master of illusion. Did I mention shady? "Well, gosh, tonight at seven? I don't think I can make it."

"You certainly can." Sylvia turned on me and I saw the sparkle in her eye. "You need to get out of the house and have some fun." Her perfectly groomed eyebrow rose like she was daring me to argue with her. Somehow, I didn't think that would be wise. "That's very generous of you, Mr. Stark, and we would love to come to your show tonight."

I cocked my head and shrugged. "Guess we'll be there."

"A woman who takes charge." He chuckled, raking his gaze over Sylvia. "I love it. Very good then. I'll save you two ladies a table up front. Just give the doorman your names when you walk in."

He bought some of the chicken jerky and other homemade treats for Mage and then, with a final wink to seal Sylvia's resolve that we were going tonight, he left.

"Down girl!" I teased her when the door closed.

She sighed. "A magician? How romantic."

"He seemed very interested in you, too."

"He did?" She feigned surprise but the little gleam in her eye told me she had been enjoying his attention too much to not have noticed his intent.

"Yes, but Sylvia, I don't know about leaving Karma alone yet."

"Oh, no," She cut me off with a wave of her hand. "You have to go." Then she weaved her arm through mine. "Karma will be fine. It'll be *muito* fun, I promise. Besides, I need you there to, you know..."

"Keep you out of trouble?"

"Exactly." She grinned.

I laughed. "All right."

TWELVE

One of my favorite things about St. Pete is you don't need a car to get around and not just because I never learned to drive. I needed the outdoors; the smell of salty night air, the winking stars, the touch of a breeze on my bare neck—food for the soul. Tonight was no exception. A fifteen minute stroll brought Sylvia and me to the front door of the theatre. We glanced at each other and I checked the address on the card again. Right place. The door sported thick coats of black shellacked paint. No windows on either side. Creepy.

"After you," I whispered.

Sylvia straightened her spine and her black cocktail dress, rested one hand on the door handle and crossed herself with the other. Then she pulled the door opened.

A burst of cold air washed over us as we stepped inside. Before us was a squatty hallway, lit only by a few wall sconces and double doors at the end, also painted black.

"Your turn." Sylvia threw me an amused smile, crossing her arms as we reached the double doors.

I pulled one open and stuck my head inside. Voices burbled low in the room and a man in a tux smiled at me. I smiled back, relieved the creepiness ended here.

"Good evening, ladies." The man in the tux glanced at a clipboard. "Do you have reservations?"

"Oh, Mr. Stark said to give you our names... Darwin and Sylvia."

"Very good. Right this way." He led us through the large room, weaving around tables to one in front of the stage. "Here you are, please look over the menu, your server will be with you shortly."

"Wow," I said, glancing around at the tables full of patrons. "I would have never known this place was here."

"Adds to the *místico*... the mystery, yes?"

"Mhm." I wasn't sure I was prepared to keep Sylvia out of the kind of trouble that gleam in her eye suggested.

"Oh, hey!" Sylvia nodded behind me. "That's Frankie Maslow, blonde lady, gold dress, two tables over."

I twisted around in my seat. The table candles kept the room dimly lit, but Frankie was still easy to spot. She sparkled in a sequined gold dress, diamonds on her neck and arms catching the light every time she laughed or raised her glass to her lips. On one side of her sat a skinny guy, his dark hair pulled back in a pony tail, wearing a white t-shirt and tux jacket with rolled up sleeves and the other side sat her red-headed assistant, who had brought the puppies into the boutique. Her assistant's black dress scooped low, showing off ample cleavage and a tattoo. I couldn't make out what the tattoo was from this far away.

I turned back to Sylvia. "Can you introduce us after the show?"

"Yes, of course."

A waitress came over and took our order right before a spotlight lit up the stage in front of us. A man stepped into the light.

"Ladies and Gentlemen, welcome to a magical evening with Landon Stark! We just ask that you sit back, enjoy your dinner and open your mind!"

The spotlight disappeared and fog rolled onto the stage. Even this filled me with a sense of expectation and adventure. This was, after all, my first magic show.

A rumbling—like far away thunderstorms— began, building until the whole room vibrated with the sound. A fast drum roll, then a loud crack of cymbals and multiple spotlights scanned the stage, crisscrossing each other as if searching for something. The waitress slipped our drinks onto the table. Two young women dropped from the ceiling, mirrors of each other in silver leotards, blonde hair slicked back into tight buns. Between them, they held a black satiny cape. I took a sip of my wine as they let the cape flutter to the stage. Yum, crisp and fruity. Whoa! The cape suddenly rose off the floor and took the shape of a person. The girl on the right, with one hand poised on her hip, grabbed the cape with her free hand and ripped it from the air.

There stood Landon Stark.

Applause erupted. Sylvia and I shared an impressed smile while we applauded with the crowd.

And that began what turned out to be a seriously cool two hours of illusions and great food. Including a memorable moment where Mage appeared from an empty box, with a rose in his mouth, and proceeded to jump off the stage and drop it in Sylvia's lap... then did a little doggie bow. Yeah, she was a goner.

After the show, Landon himself came and sat at our table, faithful Mage lying at his feet.

"That was just amazing!" Sylvia clapped. "Simply *extraordinário!*" She picked up the rose and pressed it to her nose, glancing down at Mage. "And *muito obrigada*, thank you, Mr. Mage, for the beautiful rose."

Landon smiled, his head tilting in a subtle bow. "I'm so glad... and honored that you ladies could make it this evening. Darwin? How did you enjoy the show?"

"Oh, it was magnificent! And not just because it was my first magic show ever. I mean, it really blew me away. The part where you put the two girls... are they twins by the way?"

"Yes. Tammy and Tonya."

"I thought so. So, when you put the two of them in that tiny box and only one popped back out... I was worried there for awhile until she showed back up in the end." Okay, I realized I had downed three glasses of wine and was chattering away like a squirrel. I pressed my lips together and nodded. "Great job."

He chuckled, signaling for the waitress to bring him a drink. "That's a very enthusiastic review, Darwin, thank you." He let his dark eyes focus on Sylvia, who finished up the last of her frozen, milky umbrella drink. He was about to say something, but a voice behind me interrupted him.

"Landon! Wonderful show as always."

Landon stood to greet Frankie Maslow with a two cheeked kiss. "Good evening, Frankie."

Now that she stood closer, I could see the powdered wrinkles and gray root line that revealed her true age.

Her assistant recognized me. "Darwin, right? From the pet shop?"

Boutique. Pet boutique. Oh, the tattoo was a rose with a drop of blood falling between her cleavage from a single thorn. Oops, was I staring? "Yes, I'm sorry. I didn't catch your name before?"

"Maddy."

"Maddy." Maddy had dark circles that she tried to cover with a shade yellower than her skin tone. Her hands were trembling. "Nice to see you again. How are the pups doing?"

"They're good. Sleeping through the night like babies. Thanks for your help." At least they were getting some sleep. Looked like Maddy needed a bottle of her own flower essence.

Frankie smiled down at me with perfectly white, squared off teeth and more than a little curiosity. "Hello, I'm Frankie Maslow."

I raised my hand, managing to keep myself from commenting on the size of the three rings. Seriously, how did she hold that hand up? "Darwin Winters." I motioned to Sylvia. "And you know Sylvia. She's co-owner of Darwin's Pet Boutique."

"Hey, Frankie." Sylvia waved.

"Oh, good to see you, Sylvia. So, you met my new babies? Aren't they just precious?"

"Oh yes!" We both said at once.

"I'm being rude," she flung her hand to her chest. "Everyone, this is my boyfriend, Vick Bruno." She lovingly placed a palm on his arm.

He nodded as we said our hellos, his arms never uncrossing from his chest. Yeah, I could see why Mad Dog didn't like him. He was closed off, protective and kind of rude. What was Frankie doing with a guy like him? Surely she could reel in a better fish with the kind of bait she now had. My mom used to say love is a mystery. I was beginning to understand what she meant.

I was also starting to get worried about leaving Karma alone for so long but I really wanted to talk to Frankie about some fund raising ideas.

While Frankie and Landon were exchanging pleasantries, the twins appeared, their silver outfits swapped for street clothes. They looked about in their early twenties. Stocky girls.

Gymnasts maybe? One of them waved at Frankie and then Vick made a jerking motion with his head. They followed him to the corner of the stage. I kept glancing over at them and noticed Frankie doing the same, concern pinching the corners of her eyes. At one point, one of the twins threw up her hands and laughed. Vick had his hands on his hips. He didn't look amused. This seemed to get Landon's attention, too and his eyes narrowed for a second before he went back to his conversation with Frankie.

The twins turned and walked away, leaving Vick staring after them. What in the world? What would two young girls have to talk to someone like Vick about? Maybe it was just my naivety again, but something didn't feel right about it.

When a lull in the conversation came between Frankie and Landon, I butted in. "Excuse me, Frankie?"

"Yes?" That wide smile again. I pushed the image of a camel out of my head.

"Do you have a business card? I'd like to discuss a few fund raising ideas I have for the homeless. I thought maybe we could do something together?"

"Oh, wonderful idea." She dug through a gold bag and handed me a card. She seemed genuinely pleased with the idea, which made me happy. Something got accomplished this evening besides being wowed by Landon Stark. I glanced at Sylvia. Well, for me at least. She seemed as wowed as a gal can get.

The evening wrapped up about an hour later with Landon lingering over Sylvia outside the building, asking her if she was sure she didn't want a ride home. To her credit, she refused, saying she was going to walk back with me. I watched this exchange with open curiosity but they didn't seem to notice. I couldn't figure out why she was acting so uninterested when I knew exactly how interested she was. Was this what they called "playing hard to get"?

Sylvia offered her hand, which he kissed and then she slipped her arm in mine and we walked away. I glanced back once. Landon Stark still stood there—hands in his pockets, a slight smile on his face—watching us. I rested my head wearily on Sylvia's shoulder.

THIRTEEN

I thought Karma had behaved himself quite nicely last night as he greeted me with a slight thumping tail on the bed—although extra slobber did grace my pillow, which I'm sure he did on purpose. Until the morning when I found the French doors to the porch wide open and the bowl of dog rose water emptied.

"That was naughty," I said, making sure the doors were tightly closed this time. "Don't most dogs just drink out of the toilet bowl?" He sat by the front door with his head hanging. "Well, I hope you don't get a belly ache." I sighed, reaching for my straw bag. I wasn't sure what the effects would be of so much undiluted essence. "Let's go."

I decided the time had come to go back to our morning breakfast routine at Hooker Tea Company. So, after a quick walk in the park with an extra large poop bag, he waited patiently as I mopped the wood floors of the boutique, put some fresh homemade treats in the display case, and straightened out some collars and t-shirts left in disarray. Then we headed out the door.

A twinge of sadness twisted my gut as we approached our favorite table. Did Karma feel it, too?

"You wait here, boy." I lifted a chair and placed the end of his lead around the leg. I wasn't delusional. I knew the chair would just go with him if he decided to go anywhere. This was more for the peace of mind of the people walking by who were leery of a hundred and fifty pound dog sitting there alone.

At the counter, I had to fight a big old lump in my throat when I ordered only one ham and cheese omelet. I wasn't prepared for these little things that kept fashioning the loss of my friend into sharp edges once again. I ordered Mad Dog a black tea, just in remembrance. It made me feel better.

"Excuse me," I said, trying to make it back through the small knot of customers with my tray. I was learning to pay attention to people in my space: adapting. That was the name of the game, wasn't it? Adapting to change, good or bad.

"Oh," I stopped short at the table. "Hey." Detective Blake was leaning down, two big hands scratching under Karma's ears. Karma's tongue lolled, his eyes squinted in pleasure.

"Hi, Miss Winters." He stood, dusted off his slacks and hands and smiled. Good god in heaven, the man had an electric smile. "How's he adjusting to his new arrangements?"

"Fine." I set the tray down and then slid Karma's plate in front of him. "Took him a few days to eat. He was in a real funk. Then I took him back to visit Pirate City."

"You what?"

I slid into a chair and stirred the honey into my tea. Should I have not told him that? It wasn't against the law. Still, he was making me feel like I did something wrong with the way he was staring at me like I was crazy. "It was fine. The people there were friendly and it seemed to help Karma." I snuck a glance at him as he slid into the chair across from me and folded his hands together. His crisp sapphire shirt matched his eyes. Holy moly, it was hot this morning.

"Listen, Miss Winters..."

"Darwin." Why did everyone insist on making me feel like my mother?

"Darwin. I don't know where you came from..."

Same planet as you. "Savannah."

"Okay. But, here, you can't just go wandering into the homeless camp. It's not a safe place; there are drug abusers, criminals, very, very desperate people who wouldn't think twice about robbing you... or worse. Do you understand?"

"Yes." I poured raw sugar into Mad Dog's tea, like he liked it, and stirred. There was no way I was giving up on finding out who took Mad Dog away from us, and that was something I knew I had to make Detective Blake understand. "It's a shocking way for human beings to live. And I did notice the violence. There was a boy there that looked injured just like Mad Dog. Someone is beating these poor people up. Like they don't have enough problems."

"All right, look." Detective Blake rubbed the space between his eyes and sighed. I noticed a distinct lack of a wedding band. Gah! Stop it, Darwin. This heat was really getting to me. "Since I have a feeling you're not going to listen to anything I tell you, I'll tell you this as a warning. Last month a guy named Harold Barber got released from jail. He's homeless, though I don't think he stays at Pirate City. They call him Scary Harry."

Sounded like a Sesame Street character to me. I imagined him with purple fur and big black eyebrows.

"He's a really, really dangerous guy, Darwin. We've been trying to keep tabs on him but he's slippery. If it turns out Matthew Fowler's death was not a suicide—"

"Matthew Fowler?"

"Yes. That was Mad Dog's real name."

I let this sink in. Matthew Fowler. I knew his real name now, which was something.

"If it turns out his death was a homicide, we'll look to him first." He shook his head slightly. "And I'm not telling you this to fuel your need to find out what happened to your friend. You stay away from the guy." He paused and his eyes moved to the street. "Can I ask you something?"

"You're the detective." I shrugged and sipped my tea.

"What was the nature of your relationship with Mr. Fowler?"

It took me a second to realize he was asking about Mad Dog. "He was my friend. I told you that."

"That's all? Just friends?"

Whoa. Was he asking as a detective? Something in his tone, almost embarrassment, told me it wasn't just a professional question. I decided to be honest with him. Well, as honest as I could be.

"I didn't have many friends in Savannah, detective. My sisters and I were sort of sheltered growing up—homeschooled, that sort of thing." Boy, was that an understatement. "Besides my business partner, Sylvia, at the boutique, Mad Dog was the first friend I made here. Homeless or not, he had a good heart. He loved this dog and took care of him the best he could. And Karma loved him. That tells you a lot about a person. Yeah, he was messed up from his military service, but he was nice. I enjoyed his company. He didn't deserve to have his life taken away so soon."

Detective Blake leaned back in the chair. "You really believe he was murdered, don't you?"

"Yes."

"Why? I mean, besides the fact that you don't think he fell off the wagon? What makes you so certain?"

Because Karma showed me parts of what really happened that night, shared his fear and rage with me. I took a bite of my croissant to give myself a moment to think.

He was giving me a chance to convince him. I had a feeling he wanted to believe me, but his was a profession based on facts, not hunches. I wiggled in the chair; my legs sticky with sweat. He must have seen the struggle in my face because he leaned forward again, his eyes catching mine and the rest of our surroundings disappeared. I swallowed hard.

"Go on, Darwin. If you know something you can trust me with it."

Yeah, I knew I could trust him. With real information. I could trust him to do the right thing with a solid lead. But, I couldn't trust anybody with knowledge of my gift. It only provoked fear and malice. I had learned that lesson well and was not going to screw up the chance I had to start over, in a new city, with people who thought I was a normal business owner. Nope. No matter how much he opened himself up, giving me a chance. I couldn't do it.

"I just knew Mad Dog, that's all."

He leaned back and nodded. I could sense the disappointment coming off of him in waves. Suddenly I wasn't hungry any more. I had never gotten images from people but I did feel their emotions. In this case, I wasn't sure where his disappointment started and mine ended.

"Well, time for me to open up the boutique." I gathered our plates and cups onto the tray. I could still feel his eyes on me. He expected something from me. But what? The truth, probably. He knew I was holding back. I snuck a glance at him as I reached down for Karma's plate. The muscle in his jaw twitched like he was chewing on something. Yeah, he knew.

FOURTEEN

I sat under one of the oversized red umbrellas at the Moon Under Water restaurant waiting for Frankie Maslow. She had agreed to dinner tonight to discuss some fund raising ideas for the homeless. Karma was stretched out on the brick walkway between my chair and a large white lion statue. It was a gorgeous tropical evening, still hot enough to be grateful for the tall fans circulating the air around the tables. I slipped my sunglasses off as the sun sank low enough off the bay that I didn't need them. It had been a good day. I settled into contentment as I studied the menu. Everything looked delicious. What was I in the mood for? Something spicy. Yeah, being outside in the heat made me crave spicy food.

The waitress approached wearing a red shirt and kaki's. "Hi, Can I start you off with a drink?"

"Oh, sure, I'll have a glass of Guinness. I'm waiting on someone to order dinner, though."

"No problem, I'll bring that right out."

A band played on the porch of the hotel next door. I could still hear bits of conversation going on around me. A few minutes later, I spotted

Frankie strutting down the sidewalk and had to smile at her eclectic way of dressing. She received a fair amount of attention in her zebra striped pants, which hugged her amble figure, a white tank top studded with red and black sequins and a red straw hat.

I waved her over.

"Darwin!" She air kissed my cheeks as I stood to greet her. "I'm so glad you called." Her perfect square teeth had a smear of red lipstick. I found myself running my tongue across my own teeth.

The waitress came up behind her and smiled. "Oh, hey, Frankie. What can I get for you tonight?"

"Hi, Amanda. Just bring us a bottle of your best Bourdeaux, sugar. And a couple of those rock shrimp appetizers for starters." She fell into the chair across from me with a loud sigh. "I should have gone for a massage today. Oh, I've got the best girl." She rubbed a shoulder with a plump hand. "Veronica Wilkens. You have to come with me one day, Darwin. You won't find a gal with better hands."

"Oh." I cleared my throat. I'd never had a massage before. "Sure. That'd be nice."

"So, how did you enjoy Landon Stark's show? Isn't he just amazing?" She leaned forward and lowered her voice. Her perfume smelled expensive. "Sometimes I think he's the real thing... you know, really magic. Some of things he does." She shook her head. "Damn near impossible, I'll tell ya."

Huh. She believed in real magic? Interesting. My mind wandered for a moment, imagining I could share some of the things I knew with her. Then I shook it off. Somehow I didn't imagine she would be good at keeping secrets. Taking a sip of the frothy beer, I decided I better get down to business.

"So, I heard that you're involved in working with the homeless around here, taking meals to Mirror Park every Sunday?"

"Mhm. Oh, these just look delicious," she said as Amanda slid the appetizers in front of us and opened the bottle of Bordeaux. "Yepper. I used to be one of the homeless, you know. Lived in Pirate City and everything. The way I see it, I won that lottery for the homeless community, not just me. Gotta take care of our family, right? Of course," she held up a hand as she chewed on a rock shrimp. "I never imagined the perks that would come with having money. I mean, it's not just not worrying anymore where your next meal is coming from. It's not having to feel embarrassed, it's feeling safe, it's having people look at you like you're a human being, for cripes sake, instead of ignoring you or being scared of you cause you haven't had a place to shower for weeks." She paused to take a large swallow of red wine. I could see her struggling with the anger still, the hurt. I tried to guard myself from the waves of sadness washing over me, but they rolled in strong and squeezed my chest. I stayed silent, hoping it would help her to talk it out. She forced a smile. "I mean, don't get me wrong. I believe you learn something from every experience. Being homeless taught me humility, taught me to be humble. Helped me to see inside people, beyond their disabilities or current situations. We are all brothers and sisters. All the same inside."

I raised my mug. "Amen, Frankie."

She looked sheepish as she clinked glasses. "I'm sorry. I know I get preachy sometimes."

"Not at all. Sounds like you have a lot to share with people from your experiences."

We spent the next hour or so sharing our ideas for a fundraiser, laughing and munching on the wonderful food she kept ordering. I did sneak in an order for some vegetable curry to satisfy my need for something spicy. At one point, Karma stretched and stood up beside me, sniffing the table. I noticed Frankie startle.

"You hungry, Karma?" I offered him a sausage roll. "This is Karma, he's harmless." I smiled at Frankie.

She held a hand to her chest. "Scared me, I didn't know you had a dog back there." Then her eyes narrowed. "He looks familiar."

"Yeah, you might have seen him around with his former owner, Mad Dog. He was homeless, killed a few weeks ago."

Frankie wiped her mouth with the cloth napkin, succeeding in wiping off her lipstick in the process. She looked pale. "Oh, yeah. I heard about that. The suicide? Now I recognize Karma."

"Yeah, he's been really depressed. Loved Mad Dog to pieces. He's doing better now." I rubbed his head. He was staring at Frankie like he recognized her, too. "But, you know, I don't believe he committed suicide."

"You don't? Why not?"

"Well, for one, the police think he got drunk and drowned. But, I know Mad Dog wouldn't drink. He had gotten sober for Karma."

"Huh." She finished off her glass of wine and poured another. "For a dog? That's unusual. Anything else makes you suspicious?"

I almost felt like I could confide in her. Almost. "I don't know. I spent some time with him the week he died and well, there is the fact that he kept showing up with injuries, bruises and hurt ribs. Someone was hurting him and he wouldn't go to the police."

Frankie nodded in understanding. "There's one thing you have to realize, Darwin. When you're homeless, the police aren't your friend. Their job is to keep us out of the way, as invisible as possible." She waved a piece of pita bread at me. "In fact, I wouldn't be surprised if it was the police who were beatin' on him. There's a unit that deals with street crimes got a couple of bad apples on it. I had run-ins with 'em myself. Mean suckers."

"Really?" I couldn't imagine. I guess it would make sense if that were the case. That's why he wouldn't go to the police. "Do you know their names? I've got a friend... well, acquaintance I guess, that could maybe look into it?"

She shook her head. "Your best bet, sugar, is just to stay out of it. You don't want those cops on your bad side. They can make a person disappear and make it look like their idea."

Like Mad Dog. I sighed and glanced around. Night had fallen and the tables around us were beginning to empty out. Why did everyone's advice have to be "stay out of it"? I wish that were an option. It wasn't.

FIFTEEN

An afternoon thunderstorm forced people off the streets for a bit and pushed them into the Beach Drive shops and restaurants to wait it out. A few of our customers stood chatting in front of the window, not willing to brave the downpour that was sending water gushing down the street. Sylvia stood beside Nelly Michaels and fluffed out her bichon's bangs like a proud hairdresser. I heard her laugh. "Hey, Darwin?"

I was perched on the stool behind the counter, watching gray sheets of rain tumble out of the sky. "Yes?"

"Nelly and the girls want to know what kind of fragrance we sprayed in here to make it smell so good?"

Oh geeze. I glanced back at Karma and then held up my hands. "It's um... Eu da dog rose." This sent Sylvia into peals of laughter. Karma pushed himself off his bed and came over to rest his head on my lap. "It's okay, boy." I smoothed the wrinkles in his brow. "It could have been worse. You could have drunk skunk water."

The phone rang, almost bringing me out of my skin.

Heavens on a hilltop, I was going to have to start bathing in flower essence to take care of these frazzled nerves. "Darwin's Pet Boutique."

"Hi, is this Miss Winters... ah, Darwin?"

"Yes?"

"This is Detective Blake."

"Oh," My heart did a tiny flip. I pushed a hand through my hair, trying to tame the short waves as if he could see me. "Hi, detective. What can I do for you?"

"Actually, I have some information for you. Thought it might help you get some closure with the loss of your friend. We were given a note last night that was found at Pirate City." He paused. "It was a suicide note. Signed by Mad Dog."

What?! No. no. no. That was not possible. I glanced down at Karma, stretched out on his side on the giant pillow bed Sylvia had bought for him. Or was it possible? Could Mad Dog really have decided death was better than the life he had with Karma? I mean, he was homeless. What kind of life was it really? So, why was suicide so hard for me to believe?

"Darwin? Are you still there?"

"Yeah." I felt numb. Confused. "Yes. I'm here." A flash of lightning lit up Beach Drive. A deep rumble rolled through on its heels. This news brought up more questions than answers for me. It made me doubt myself and it made me doubt Mad Dog. And that made me feel like a stone had dropped from my heart into my stomach. I had to get off the phone so I could breathe. "Okay. I... I appreciate you letting me know, detective. Thank you." I hung up. Now what?

"Sylvia, I'm going to go get us some lunch." I heard my voice but felt disconnected from it.

Sylvia glanced up from straightening the collars. Her noon appointment was late. "You want to wait a few moments, the storm will go away?"

"No. I'll be fine." I pulled the umbrella out from beneath the counter. "French onion soup from Cassis?"

"Sure."

I felt her concern as I left, but she didn't push me for information, which I appreciated because I had no idea what I could say. I had no idea how I felt about this new piece of information. Except sad and maybe a bit angry. And confused. Yeah, definitely that.

The sidewalk was already flooded so my flip flops squished with each step. I didn't bother with the umbrella so my hair and cotton dress both clung to me as I pushed through the rain. The tiny needles of chilly rain gave me something to focus on, something to feel besides numb. It was a welcome distraction.

I leaned against the wall outside after I placed my order, protected from the storm by the building's architecture but shivering from being soaked to the bone already. I watched the rain splash on the wide sidewalk, on the row of green umbrellas over empty tables lined up against Beach Drive. I should have asked what the note said exactly. Would he have been able to tell me? And who gave it to them? Mad Dog's tent had a new owner. Why didn't they find it sooner? His back pack had gone missing, so they didn't get it from there. Unless they had found his back pack? That's the most likely place he would have left a note... if he did, in fact, leave one. Okay, if they found the back pack, maybe there was something else in it, some other clue as to what was going on in his life at the time of his death. That's it. I had to go back to Pirate City and find out.

***

We closed at six and I was on my way to Pirate City by six forty-five, Karma by my side, a Ziploc bag full of ice cold, lemon cookies in my pack for G. I probably should have waited until the weekend, when I had more than an hour and a half before night fall, but I felt like the more time that went by, the more likely Mad Dog's death would get lost in the system.

What if I couldn't figure out what happened? What if he was murdered and that person was just walking the streets? I pedaled faster, glancing back to make sure Karma was keeping up. I had to smile at his wide lope, tongue flapping beside his jaw. He really was a sweet boy.

I parked my bike against the tree under the No Trespassing sign and walked into the camp.

"Hey there, Snow White." Pops chuckled. He was playing cards with Minnie and two others I didn't recognize. Another group hung out in broken lawn chairs, passing around a joint with a tiny glowing tip.

I waved. "Hey, guys."

"Oh, hi, nice lady!" G appeared and ambled toward me clutching a shoebox. "You brought some cookies?"

"Hi, G. Yes, I brought some cookies." I pulled the Ziploc bag from my pack and handed it over to G. He cradled the shoebox as if it were breakable and accepted the bag. I noticed his hand shaking.

"What's in the box, G?"

He didn't answer me, just nodded with a big old toothless grin and walked away. Probably for the best I didn't know anyway.

I moved closer to the table. "Is Mac here?"

"Yeah, he's in his office." Pop paused from organizing his cards and motioned to the large blue tarp to my right.

"Thanks." I headed that way with Karma at my heels. The tarp did offer some shade but it was still hot as Hades under there. Probably a lot more humid, too. I stepped inside, being careful not to trip on the rug that had begun to rot and mingle with the soil. "Hi, Mac." Mac sat at a table and glanced up at me from the paper in his hand.

"Couldn't stay away, eh?" he snorted. His attention went back to the paper. "What can I do ya for, Snow White?"

Wow. Didn't take long for a nickname to stick around here. I glanced at the man who sat across from him. I didn't recognize him from my last visit. He didn't seem too interested in what I was there for so I just came out with it.

"The police said someone from here turned in a suicide note from Mad Dog. That true?"

Mac hesitated then he put down the paper and folded his hands. "Hey, give me and this lady a minute, Hops. We'll finish up your resume in a bit." The guy stood and left without a fuss. "Have a seat." He motioned to the chair the guy just left.

"You know there are three sides to every story, right?"

I took a seat. "I just want the truth."

He sighed. "The truth is... you really need to stay on your side of town."

I crossed my arms and waited. That wasn't what I came here to hear.

"Look. It's obvious you cared about Mad Dog but it's also obvious that you don't have a damn clue what real life is about. Mad Dog probably considered you a friend, too so I'm gonna do him a favor and tell you the only thing I can. Stop asking questions. Go home."

I stared at him hard. Real life? What does that even mean? That my life isn't real just because it's not as hard as his?

"I may not know what life is like here in a homeless camp. I may not understand the full breadth of the suffering that goes on here but I do know that it's not right to ignore a friend when they need you. And whether Mad Dog is alive or not, he needs me. And Karma needs me. And I'm not walking away from either of them until I've seen justice done. If someone killed him, he deserves to have that someone pay for it."

"Je-sus, girl." Mac shook his head and his face reddened. "You want to go and get yourself killed then go on. Just don't involve us, we got enough heat."

"So, that's it? You're not going to answer my question about the letter?"

"No, I'm not." Mac leaned back and crossed his arms. "And it's gonna get dark soon, you best be on your way."

I glanced over at the sun, now just a melted orange puddle on the horizon.

"Fine." I stood up and Karma stood with me. "Will you just tell me if y'all found his back pack?"

He started to say something and then just shook his head, pressing his lips together. "Nope."

"Thank you." Not that his answer helped much. I wasn't sure now he would tell me if they did.

As Karma and I emerged from the path, a white police cruiser made a three point turn at the dead end. It pulled up beside us and the passenger side window slid down.

"Evening ma'am."

"Evening, officer." A low growl started in Karma's throat and I glanced down at him. He had gone stiff, the fur standing up on the back of his spine. I'd never seen him act like this before and it worried me. There was no way I could stop him if he decided to attack somebody and good heavens please don't let him attack a police officer. They'd put him down for sure. "It's okay boy." I reached down and placed a steadying hand on his back.

"This isn't a very safe part of town for a young lady. Can I ask what you're doing here?"

I could still feel Karma bristling under my hand, but at least he had stopped growling. "Sure," I leaned in closer and read the name on his shirt. "Officer Cruz. I was taking cookies to a friend."

"Cookies?" His dark eyes flashed with humor. "Really? In Pirate City?"

"Yes, lemon cookies." I knew it sounded ridiculous and frankly, I was enjoying that fact. He probably thought cookies were a code word for drugs. Let 'em think that.

"Hey," the officer at the wheel leaned forward and pointed at Karma. "Isn't that the dog that hung out with Mad Dog?"

"Yes, Karma." And he doesn't seem to be too fond of y'all. "You knew Mad Dog?"

"It's our job to know the homeless in the area."

But not your job to find out who murdered one of them? I couldn't see his name tag, but I tried to see his face as best as I could in the shadow of the cruiser. "Yeah, it's a real shame what happened to him, he was a nice guy. Karma really misses him. It helped bringing him back here to where he used to be with Mad Dog, I think."

This seemed to satisfy them as to why I was there. They visibly relaxed. "Well, like I said. Not a good place for a young woman. We'll make sure you get to the main road safely. Have a good evening."

The cruiser crept behind me as I pedaled back to the main road. Karma kept glancing back. What made him so upset about those two? Did he remember something?

We reached the edge of North Straub Park as the street lights flickered on. Just then, Karma took off on me, running down Fifth Avenue like his tail had caught fire. I could hear his nails on the concrete over the traffic.

"Karma!" I yelled, as I clumsily turned my bike in that direction and tried to catch up. "Karma, stop! Heel! Halt!" I knew I should have gone back for his lead when I realized I had forgotten it.

All sorts of scenarios ran through my mind... none of them good. He was heading into the old northeast neighborhood, which I was not really familiar with. I rode as fast as I dared on the sidewalk, crossing over First Street then Second; all the while squinting, checking the yards, calling to Karma.

The sidewalk opened up when I reached the Palladium Theatre. A group of people were gathered on the steps.

"Excuse me," I called. "Did anyone see a large dog run past here?"

"Yeah," a teenage girl answered, pointing. "That way."

"Thanks." I pushed off, my legs shaking from adrenalin, crossed Third Street and passed under the shadow of a large tree. Bass boomed from one of the nearby houses. The breeze carried a hint of smoke from a grill.

"Ah!" I squeezed the brakes so hard, the bike skidded to a stop. Right in front of Karma.

"Karma!" I half-whispered, half-yelled. 'What are you doing?"

At the moment he was sitting on the sidewalk, staring at me with a "what took you so long" gaze. I eased the bike onto its side in the grass, just in case any other lunatic came barreling down the sidewalk in the dark, and kneeled beside him. I still didn't have a leash, so I was going to have to talk him into coming back with me.

"Okay, Karma. You and me are going to have to get one thing straight." I stroked him under his slobbery chin. "There will be no running off, especially at night... especially when I'm too tired to chase you."

He gave a low huff and stared straight ahead. I followed his gaze and my heart felt like somebody just tried to jump start it with raw electricity. There, behind a row of scrawny bushes, sat the townhouse. I stared back at Karma. It couldn't be, could it?

I closed my eyes, bringing up the vision I had received from Karma the day they found Mad Dog: gray wood planks, porch with white railing in front, shuttered window above the A frame on the left, tree on the right obscuring the flat part of the roof. I had it. I opened my eyes. Yep. It was like seeing a developed photograph of the image in my mind.

Okay, if this place was involved with Mad Dog's death, then standing outside with his dog probably wasn't the safest thing to be doing. I'd have to come back without Karma. I made a mental note of the area then whispered in Karma's ear. "Okay, I got it, boy. Come on."

I gave Karma some extra blender chicken when we were tucked safely back in our townhouse. I also lit some candles and slipped into a hot bath to calm my nerves.

What triggered him to run to that house tonight? The police officers? Something at Pirate City? Well, one thing was certain, he wasn't letting go of Mad Dog's death and he trusted me to keep my promise. Suicide note or not, my investigation would continue.

SIXTEEN

"Okay, Karma, you have to stay here." I put out his breakfast of blender steak and carrots. Even though I knew I had to do this alone, the sad way he hung his head made me feel guilty for leaving him. "I'll be quick about it. I promise." I smooshed my face against his forehead and scratched under his ears. "Eat your breakfast."

Sundays were always quiet in St. Pete. Except for around the Farmer's Market, but that wasn't even open yet. I turned my bike down Fifth Avenue and headed west. It looked different in the stark light of morning sun and much easier to navigate. It wasn't long before I had come upon the Palladium Theatre, with its big banners declaring the Tampa Bay Symphony was in town. I pushed on, not exactly sure what the plan was once I got there.

The house appeared more rundown in the daytime, yet not as haunted. I slipped off my bike and started messing with the chain, all the while watching—behind dark glasses—for any signs of activity inside. All seemed quiet, though the inhabitants could just still be asleep.

I could just knock on the door and see who answered. But, what would I say? No, that would give away the only thing I had going for me—surprise. They might get suspicious, especially if they're doing something illegal. I slipped back onto my bike. I couldn't just hang out here on the sidewalk; they could be watching me right now for all I knew. I shivered at the thought. Time to move on.

I kept heading west and there—at the corner of Fourth Street—I recognized the blue pawn shop from Karma's image. And there was the Florida Bank across the street. I closed my eyes and recalled the sequence. This location was the first snapshot. The last one before the image of him jumping in the water was near a Courtyard by Marriot. I knew what this meant, but I pushed on toward Mirror Lake just to underline the fact that Karma had shown me the right house. Yep, I turned left on Fourth Street and passed the Marriot right before I hit Mirror Lake Drive. Bingo. I circled around the right side of Mirror Lake. This was the first time I'd been back since Mad Dog's death. The sounds, the smells, everything brought back the memory of that morning and the grief. I stopped and washed down the lump in my throat with some bottled water.

Okay, focus. I stared out at the glittering lake and the fountain sprouting from the center of it. I took all of Karma's images and watched them in reverse order to get the sequence of events.

So, Karma started at the house, ran down the same streets I just came down and eventually jumped into Mirror Lake to try and save Mad Dog. That meant Mad Dog was in that house without Karma. Karma must have been waiting for him outside. And Mad Dog didn't leave that place of his own accord or Karma would have been with him at that point, not running after him.

So, he died in the house and whoever killed him drove to Mirror Lake and dumped his body in the water? Yeah, that felt right. It fit. So, who lived in that house? I could probably look up the owner's name on the internet.

On my way out, I noticed people sitting under the palms near the lake and spotted a van pull in. Then I remembered. It was Sunday morning. The day Frankie Maslow brought food here for the homeless. I rode over.

"Hi, Frankie."

"Darwin!" Frankie stepped out of the van and moved around to open the back door. "What brings you out here so early?"

"Just going for a bike ride. But since I'm here, you need some help?"

"Sure thing, sugar. I could always use the extra hands."

I helped her carry boxes of sturdy plates, plastic bins, a silver pot big enough to sit in and some trash bags over to a shaded picnic table. More people started to gather between the table and the lake.

"Morning." Frankie waved to them.

"Morning, Mama Maslow." Some of them greeted her back, some just waved.

"All right, just start settin' out the plates. The scrambled eggs and ham are in the pot, that bin right there has hash browns and this one here has toast." She pulled open one of the trash bags. "Oh, and these here are oranges. Got a ton of them today."

I followed her instructions and soon the people were moving forward to get a plate of food. There was a lot of friendly banter being thrown around, which made me smile. I recognized a few of the people from Pirate City. Minnie for one—who Frankie greeted with a bear hug—and Hops, the guy Mac had been helping with a resume. Hops hardly said two words as he took his plate, eyes downcast. What was his story? My heart broke for him. I looked around for G but didn't see him.

After everyone had their plates and were seated in the grass, I walked with Frankie as she asked people how they were doing, getting the scoop on the comings and goings of the camp. I couldn't imagine how strange it must be for Frankie, to go from a homeless camp to the Vinoy. I really admired her for not forgetting about her camp mates.

We came upon the young, dark kid who I saw at Pirate City. He looked even worse now. Both eyes were puffy almost to the point of being shut and his movements suggested he was in pain. Just. Like. Mad Dog.

"Hey, Frankie." I leaned in close to her. "What do you know about that kid right there?"

"Um," she shrugged, "just that he's a pain in my arse." She glanced at me. "Why?"

"Just curious. He was hurt last time I saw him, too."

"There's lots of ways for a young man to get hurt out there on the streets." When we approached him, he glanced from Frankie to me and then back to Frankie.

I noticed needle marks along the inside of his arm. Frankie must have noticed them, too.

"You gotta get clean, Junior."

He swallowed and then shrugged. "What for?" He glanced back up at me and I detected suspicion. "Snow White. You tight wit Mama Maslow, huh? You a lover or a fighter?"

"Hey," Frankie stuck up a hand. "This is a no mouthin' off zone. Zip it."

"Ah. It's cool. I didn't know." He let his eyes wander over me. "Be somethin' to watch, though."

"Get clean, Junior, or you're not gonna survive until your next birthday." Frankie shot him a look that could've killed, then led me away.

I had no idea what that exchange was about, but I didn't like it. There seemed to be warnings squeezed between every word.

SEVENTEEN

"A date?" Sylvia turned from counting the drawer, her hand on her hip. "You have a date?"

I could hear her usual mix of curiosity and excitement. I tried to nip it in the bud.

"No, it's not really a date. He is just trying to be nice and get my mind off of Mad Dog for a day."

The "he" was Detective Blake. I had left a message for him about the townhouse, explained Karma's odd reaction to it—leaving out the psychic part, of course—and told him what I had found out. A corporation called Frat Boys, Inc. owned the townhouse but I still had no idea who lived there. Anyway, his response was to return my call and ask me if I had been to the Dali Museum. When I said I hadn't, he asked me to go with him on Saturday to "get my mind off of Mad Dog." That's not exactly a date in my book but, apparently, it is in Sylvia's.

"This detective Blake, he is handsome guy?"

I felt my cheeks burn. "Well, yeah, sure." I shrugged and busied myself with wrapping up the baked goods in wax paper while trying to force all thoughts away of his eyes or his smile or his broad shoulders or…

"Aaaaa!" Sylvia sauntered up beside me. I could actually feel her smiling at me. It was like standing next to a heat lamp. "It's about time you go out. What are you wearing?"

"Don't make me nervous about this. If I think it's a date, I'll be nervous." I'd only been on two dates before and those were two of the most humiliating days of my life.

"Okay, okay. What are you wearing on your not-date?"

I gave up. I was too tired to resist the force that was Sylvia on the subject of dating and clothes. I leaned against the counter, folded my arms and gave her a smile of surrender. "I don't know. What do you wear on a not-date date?"

She tapped her lip with a French-manicured nail. "We have no time to shop before tomorrow." This made her brow crinkle in the middle. "How about… no…" I could see her mentally shuffling through my limited wardrobe. I have always had a hard time with clothes. They have to be natural materials: organic cotton, limited dyes. My skin is very sensitive.

"Aha!" She clapped. "You wear the little sundress with rose buds. It has nice hip line, poofs out enough to give you a womanly shape."

"Hey, I have a shape!"

She raised an eyebrow. "You are a stick figure."

I tried to act indignant but she was right. "Fine." I smiled. "I'll wear the sundress. But," I held up a finger, "it's still not a date."

***

The detective and I had agreed to meet in front of the museum at noon, so I took the downtown looper bus, which drops off right in front. I could have walked, but I would have arrived sweaty. Even though this wasn't a date, I didn't want to make that kind of impression. As the bus pulled up, I saw the detective standing there waiting. Prompt. I appreciated that.

It's not a date. It's not a date. I mashed my lips together, trying to smooth out the rose pink gloss Sylvia had suggested I put on. He was wearing jeans and a lemon yellow polo shirt. He looked like a model straight out of a Sears catalog. Here we go. I shouldered my straw bag and took a calming breath.

"Enjoy your visit, ma'am." The driver said, as I dropped a few extra quarters through the slot.

There's that ma'am again. "Thank you."

"Hi." He smiled down at me and seemed so relaxed, I actually felt my own anxiety unwinding.

"Hi there. This is something." I glanced up at the strange building. "I'm sure there's a story as to why there's glass bubbles wrapped around the museum like fish eyes?"

"Yep." He turned so he could point to the first bubble. "That one is called the Enigma, named after one of Dali's paintings. It's like a giant sky light. The other bubble is called the Igloo, for obvious reasons. The building itself has eighteen inch thick concrete walls and can withstand a Category 5 hurricane."

"Wow. You're going to be an excellent tour guide." I grinned.

"Sorry. Just stop me if I bore you. I tend to be a detail orientated person." He rested a hand on the small of my back and motioned toward the entrance with the other. "Shall we?"

My skin warmed and tingled under his touch. Oh heavens. I repeated my "this is not a date" mantra as we entered the museum straight into the belly of the beast—a large gift shop.

"They don't mess around, do they?" I eyed a large replica of Dali's famous melting pocket watch hanging from the edge of a table stacked with colorful t-shirts. The air conditioner blasted welcomed cool air as we navigated our way around the merchandise.

"Two adults, please," Detective Blake said to the lady behind the counter.

Oh no. He paid for me. Did that mean this *was* a date?

"Er, thanks," I said as he motioned for me to get my wristband.

As we began our ascent up the double helix staircase, which spiraled skyward in the middle of the museum, I glanced upward into the glass and aluminum ceiling. "How high up is that?"

"About 75 feet."

"Any reason in particular the exhibit is way up there?" I wasn't in bad shape but, by the time we hit the second floor, my thighs burned in protest.

"Yep. Weeds out the wimps." His laugh tickled my insides. I couldn't help but grin at him.

"And you're a comedian, too."

"Sorry, the art is on the third floor to protect it in case of flooding."

"Ah," I said, "that makes sense." Almost to the top.

"So, are you a Dali fan?"

"I like some of his stuff more than others. His surrealist work is great. Not as fond of the work he did after he moved to the US, the science and religious pieces." We finally arrived at the top. It was a breathtaking view of the gulf. "Whew."

"That tells me a lot about you." Detective Blake chuckled behind me.

I whirled around. "What does?"

"The kind of art you prefer."

"Oh, really?" I crossed my arms. "And what exactly does it tell you about me?"

He was staring at me. "You know, in the sunlight, your eyes are violet?"

I started to say something, but stammered and then managed to choke out a weak, "Don't change the subject." This moved his mouth into a slow, seductive smile. I was suddenly aware of the blood pulsing through my veins, of the evenness of his breath and the glassy, crystal nature of his eyes.

A lady with a cane bumped into me in her effort to get around us. We broke eye contact, both turning away sheepishly.

"Come on," he cleared his throat. "The art awaits."

"Whoa," I breathed as we entered the door and turned right, finding walls and walls of Dali's work. "This is like stumbling into someone else's dream life, nightmares and all."

We wound our way through the different sections in awed silence. There were oils and watercolors, drawings and photographs. Even sculptures. Whether you liked the man or not, you had to admire the volume of work he turned out in one lifetime.

I stopped in front of Archeological Reminiscence of Millet's Angelus, one of my favorites. I was aware of the detective close behind me as a warm presence.

Dali's giant depiction of the farmer and his wife always made me think of aliens. "He claimed the two peasants in the original Millet painting were mourning over the grave of their dead child. And then later, when Millet's painting was x-rayed, they did see the dark shape of a coffin under layers of paint." This was one of the first things that intrigued me about the artist during our home studies of him. He seemed so in touch with the invisible, the unconscious, the unknown. Like he was a conduit for things he could pull from the universe—secret things. "Do you think he had some secret power?" I asked. Yeah, this was a test. Would he scoff? "Like some psychic ability?"

"No."

My heart sank a little. He didn't laugh, but he didn't hesitate either. Obviously set in his beliefs.

"He was just a master at confusing reality and unreality."

I wasn't ready to give up. "How do we even know what's real and what's some grand illusion that we're playing a part in?"

"Exactly his point, I think."

I wanted to ask him a more pointed question about whether he believed in psychic abilities but what if he asked me what I believed? I'd have to lie or, at least, change the subject. Uncomfortable either way. If I wanted him to see me as normal, I'd have to let it go.

Two hours immersed in the mind of Dali was about all I could take. I was emotionally drained, so when Detective Blake suggested lunch, I agreed.

We took the looper over to the Pier and headed up to the rooftop restaurant, Cha Cha Coconuts.

"Sit out on the deck?"

"Sure."

A live band played some Jimmy Buffet song as we took a table beneath the shade. It felt good to sit down, a breeze blowing and the blue gulf water below us. I lifted up the plastic spray bottle next to the ketchup. Somebody had written 'Bird B Gone" on it in black marker. I glanced around at the sea gulls and pigeons keeping their distance on the outskirts of the tables and smiled. "That's funny."

"Yeah, you have to get creative with the birds around here or they'll take over the place one French fry at a time."

The waitress came over, and after the detective's insistence that I try "the best fish tacos on the planet," we ordered and then he leaned forward on the table and stared at me. I squirmed. His stare could cut a diamond. I figured he must have honed it for interrogation purposes.

"So, how're things going with the new pet boutique?"

"Mm, great. Wonderful, actually. Better than we had planned for. Sylvia's booked up weeks in advance and we're learning the specialty stuff really moves in this area, like the homemade treats, aromatherapy oils, flower essence. Pet owners really seem to want their pets to be happy, not just healthy." I thought about Karma. It was true. I wanted so much for him to be happy. Detective Blake must have read my mind.

"And how's the big guy doing? Karma. Feeling better?"

I wanted to say "he'll feel much better when you catch Mad Dog's killer," but I managed to bite my tongue. Literally. Thank heavens the waitress came back with iced water, which I promptly held on my throbbing tongue. I gave a tight smile, swallowed and then said, "He'th fine."

Detective Blake did a little double take and then sipped his coke, while I pretended to be interested in the discarded straw wrapper on the deck until my face stopped burning.

Once I felt my mouth was in working order again, I tested it out. "So, did you find out anything more about the townhouse?"

He cocked his head and then nodded as if he just remembered what I was asking about. "I haven't looked into it, no."

My heart sank. He wasn't taking this seriously. Of course, I knew he had a million other things to do on his job, but still. "You don't think it's odd that a corporation owns the place?"

"Not really. A lot of corporations are set up to invest in the real estate market, especially after the market crashed. They probably bought up a bunch of property for rental houses, hoping to sell if, and when, the market picks back up."

"Is there any way to find out who's renting it?"

He sighed. "I think you missed your calling, Darwin. You should have been a detective."

The waitress put our plates down in front of us. The tacos did smell delicious but I didn't want to let go of this topic. I wasn't above pouting, either. It seemed to work.

"All right." He picked up a taco and gave me a smile. It was half resignation, half irritation. "I'll look into it for you if you promise me you're going to stop poking around in dangerous places like Pirate City."

I crossed my fingers under the table. "Deal."

Shaking his head, he bit off a generous bite of taco, chewed, swallowed and then looked at me again. "So, I take it you don't believe Mr. Fowler actually wrote that suicide note?"

"No, I'm sorry, I don't." I bit into my taco. Wow. Mmm. This was amazing!

"Why?"

Does there have to be a reason for everything with this man? Maddening. I finished chewing as I stared at the band and tried to put together a reason. They were actually pretty impressive.

"Detective Blake—"

"Will."

"Will I what?"

"No, call me Will. It's my first name."

"Ohhh." I grinned. "Wait... William? As in William Blake, after the poet?"

"What can I say, my mother was a romantic. Just Will, though."

"Okay. Will." I adjusted my sundress under my legs so they wouldn't stick to the plastic chairs. "I can't tell you." No, *really*, I can't tell you. "I just knew him well enough to know that he would not commit suicide."

His eyes fell to his plate and a faint wave of regret washed over me. "People can surprise you, Darwin."

I'd give him that. "True." I waited until the wave subsided before I took another bite.

"They can surprise you in good ways too, though."

He let his eyes meet mine over our tacos and smiled. "True."

We finished our meal and sat for a little while listening to the band and watching a few brave souls sway around the deck to the music. I had a sudden urge to ask Will if he wanted to join them, so that's when I knew it was time to go.

"This was a really lovely day, Will, thank you. I better get back to Karma, though. He's probably hungry by now."

"All right."

Was that disappointment? I had long since figured out by the way he looked at me that he probably did consider this a date. Was this the point where I was supposed to play hard to get? Oh heavens, I should have asked Sylvia what to do when it was time to go. Shake his hand? Hug? Leave without looking back?

Turns out, by the time we rode the looper back to Beach Drive—between the tidbits he told me about the city and the kind of afternoon heat that makes for drowsy, lazy energy—I was so relaxed, I forgot all about my concerns.

When I stood up to get off the bus, he pecked me on the cheek and slipped a business card in my hand.

"That has my cell phone number on it in case you need me."

His kiss left a warm spot on my cheek and the smell of fresh rain in the air. "Thanks. I had a great time."

He smiled above me. "See you soon."

EIGHTEEN

Sunday afternoon, Karma and I were crossing North Straub Park with a backpack full of goodies when I spotted Frankie Maslow pushing a leopard skin pet stroller down the sidewalk. I rushed to catch up.

"Hey, Frankie." We came up beside her.

"Oh, Hey, Darwin." She glanced down at Karma, who was sniffing at the two pups through the netting. "He won't think Itty and Bitty are snacks now, will he?" She eyed him warily. The two pups started yapping and Karma tilted his head and backed up.

"No, he's just curious and looks like a bit intimidated." I laughed. "Itty and Bitty, huh? Cute." I noticed a Kleenex in her hand and red blotches on her skin under oversized sun glasses. Had she been crying? "So, what are you three up to this gorgeous morning?"

"Just taking a walk, trying to clear my head."

"Everything all right?"

"Yeah." She swiped at her nose with the Kleenex. "No. Well, it'll be fine. It's just my assistant, Maddy, she just up and quit on me yesterday. And you know, I don't understand it, she was like a daughter to me. Her family is seriously screwed up. They steal cars, run a chop shop. Just trash. I got her away from them. Gave her a chance to go to school, to have a better life." She stopped under the shade of a tree and pulled a dish and water bottle from beneath the stroller. "I tried to offer her more money but she wouldn't take it. She seemed as upset as I was. I just don't understand it."

I watched her unzip the netting, pour some water into the dish and put it in the stroller. One pup eagerly lapped at it with a postage stamp sized tongue; the other cowered in the corner, shaking and staring up at us.

"What's the matter little girl?" I reached down and stroked her head. *Zap!*

Frankie was saying something but her words got lost in the white noise of the vision: Vick was yelling, his hand squeezing someone's neck. Then I spotted the bleeding rose tattoo below his grip. Maddy!

Oh boy. Why was he choking Maddy? I started jogging in place and pumping my arms up and down until I felt the jolt of energy disburse.

"Hot flashes." I leaned over with my hands on my knees. Karma had come over and pressed himself against me. I had figured out he does this when he's worried. "It's all right, boy." I gave him a reassuring scratch.

"Hot flashes? You're a bit young for that." She zipped the netting back up. "I didn't start having those until I turned fifty. Not that fifty's that far behind me, mind you."

I needed some time with Frankie to try and get some answers. "Hey, Frankie. I was heading over to Pirate City to drop off some supplies. Want to join me? It might help get your mind off of Maddy."

"Well sure. Why not? Be good to see what the boys have done with the place."

I felt a twinge of guilt for lying to Will about staying away from Pirate City. But my sense of loyalty to Mad Dog and Karma far outweighed a small lie in my mind. As we stepped onto the well worn path, off the dead end street, I veered off the small talk, too.

"How are things going with Vick?"

"Fine, I guess. Haven't seen him an awful lot lately, though. He's pretty busy with his business and all."

"That's too bad. What does he do?"

"Um," she struggled to get the stroller over a root branch without jostling the pups. "He has a computer business, sells stuff online." She reached down and smacked her leg.

"Oh, hold on. I have bug spray." As I rustled through the stuffed back pack, I asked as casually as possible. "How do Vick and Maddy get along?"

"Oh, fine." She accepted the bug spray. "Thanks." The smell permeated the air as she sprayed herself. When she was done, she handed it back and put her hands on her hips. "You know, come to think of it, they have been acting funny around each other lately. Maddy was unusually quiet when he was around last time.

You think they had a fight? That has something to do with her leavin'?"

I shoved the spray back in and re-shouldered the pack. "I don't know but maybe it's something to ask her about?"

"Yeah. If she'll answer my calls."

As soon as we entered the clearing, I knew something was wrong. Karma stiffened and started sniffing the air. Frankie stopped beside me, listening.

"Awfully quiet."

"Yeah, too quiet."

We walked deeper into the camp and came upon the overturned table. Karma sniffed it. The hairs on my arms stood up. "Where is everyone?"

"Over here." A voice called from the tarp that served as Mac's office.

We rushed over. Frankie parked the pups beside the makeshift shelter. "What in heaven's happened here?"

"Scary Harry happened." Pops pressed a wet rag to his eye. Mac was laid out on the eroding carpet with a shirt under his head, blood drying on his nose and mouth. Minnie was trying to gingerly wash it off. "Bastard had a gun this time."

"He didn't shoot anybody, did he?" Frankie asked.

"No... not this time." Pops grunted. "Took our week's pool of money and food stamps, though."

"Don't you worry about that. I'll cover it." Frankie looked around at the smashed stuff scattered about. "Christ on Christmas, did he have to destroy everything?"

"Where is everyone?"

Minnie looked up at me. "Left. For the best. He was in some kind of mood. Probably would've killed somebody today if he had any resistance." So, they thought he was capable of murder? Maybe he had already killed.

The despair hung thick as molasses under the tarp. I had to plant my feet to keep myself from trying to escape it. Such a hot and heavy emotion. "We can get you to the hospital."

"We're fine." Mac made a motion with his hand like he was swatting a fly. With it came a whoosh of anger as a streak of red through my mind.

Kneeling down, I unzipped my back pack. "Well, maybe this'll help the pain, at least." I pulled out the icepacks. "Thought with all the injuries around here lately, y'all could use some of these." Squeezing it firmly to activate the cold, I handed it to Minnie.

"Thanks." She held it to Mac's jaw.

The smell, the heat and the emotional overload were getting to me. Tiny black stars popped in my vision. My first thought was to call the police. But my second thought was of the two officers I had met and Frankie's warning about not being able to trust some of them. Well, I could trust Will. Maybe he could do something about this Scary Harry situation. We turned as rustling and voices reached us.

The people were filtering back in from their hiding places in the woods. I stood up and helped Frankie, who was trying to clean up the scattered and broken belongings. We both grabbed an end of the plywood that served as Mac's desk and set it back on the bricks. I unpacked the rest of the items I had brought and put them on the plywood.

"If you make a list for us, we can bring stuff you need." I pulled at my white cotton tank; sweat was gluing it to my body. Karma was sitting outside, panting hard. I had to get him out of this heat.

"How 'bout a winning lottery ticket." Mac's swollen lips made his attempt at a grin look more like a grimace.

"Glad Harry didn't knock the sense of humor loose from that thick skull of yours." Frankie shook her head. "Darwin's right. Make a list and, Minnie, you meet me in front of the Vinoy at six tonight with it. We'll take care of you." She stepped out from beneath the tarp, then turned back around. "Be sure aspirin's on there, you're gonna need it." She wrangled the pet stroller back out into the open and peeked in. "Come on, we gotta get these babies out of the heat."

Our walk back out of Pirate City was torturous. We were hot, drained and angry.

"Hey, I got an idea." Frankie's mascara had smeared under her eyes, and her skin was pasty, but her face suddenly lit up. "I'll throw a charity bash for the gang. We can do an auction, raffle off some stuff... invite all the rich folks. Be more profitable than a dog wash, right?"

"Definitely." I glanced back as we emerged onto the street, making sure Karma was still behind us. "More fun than washing dogs, too."

We laughed. It seemed to blow away some of the dark cloud. On the street, we took a break and gave everyone water. I poured some over Karma's head.

"Hey, Frankie? The morning they found Mad Dog at Mirror Lake... it was a Sunday. Don't you usually go there every Sunday? I didn't see any of those guys around." I pointed back down the trail. "Do you think they knew something about Mad Dog's death?"

"Oh," Frankie zipped up the netting and put the water away. "Well, I didn't go because Vick had called me and said not to; said there were cops everywhere and had the place roped off. I knew once the gang saw cops everywhere, they wouldn't go near the place."

Made sense. Sad that the relationship between the homeless and the police was so adversarial. Still, that didn't prove that no one in the camp knew about Mad Dog.

We started walking again.

"Isn't there someplace else these guys could stay that'd be safer?"

"You mean like a shelter? Sure. But they're already overcrowded. Besides, some of these guys have mental issues, you know. They can't live indoors."

"Yeah. Mad Dog was like that. He had PTSD, from the war."

Frankie eyed me hard. "You really cared about him, huh?"

"I didn't know him that long, but yeah. He was a kind soul. Didn't deserve to die like he did." I sighed. "The police were given a suicide note from someone in Pirate City. It was supposedly written by Mad Dog."

"You don't sound convinced."

"Honestly, Frankie, I don't know what to believe anymore. Everyone keeps telling me to drop it, to just let it go. But, what if someone killed him and covered it up? How can I let that go?"

"You have an extreme sense of loyalty, Darwin." She sounded worried. "I'm not sure that's a good thing when you pick friends like Mad Dog."

"Why? Because he was a homeless guy? You said yourself we're all the same inside."

She stopped walking, her head hanging. "You know, you're right. I did." When she lifted her head, some inner conflict had tears in her eyes. "I'll see what I can find out, all right? If there was foul play involved I..." she nodded, "I promise I'll help you bring the person responsible to justice."

I felt so grateful to her. I wasn't even sure there was anything she could do, but maybe she had connections, had access to information that came with being plugged into the area. It felt good to have someone on my side finally. "Thank you, Frankie."

"You're welcome, sugar." She pushed on. "All right, now let's talk about this party."

NINETEEN

Sunday night, while the new treats were baking, I decided Karma and I needed a little help in the tension department. The distant rumble of thunder had him pacing in front of the French doors, and the scene at Pirate City had left me feeling more than a little unsettled. I dropped my zafu cushion between the couch and coffee table and sat down with a tray of supplies: a crystal bowl half full with rain water, three moonstones, Cyprus oil, sea salt and rosemary.

Taking in a few cleansing breaths, I set my intention. If there was one thing Grandma Winters had drilled into us girls, it was the power of intention. *Grandma Winters*. I wondered if she knew I had left Savannah. She wasn't your typical cookies and bed time stories type of grandma. Nope. She visited twice a year and stayed for two weeks to help our "gifts" grow. My mother always seemed uncomfortable around her, always on her best behavior. We used to think mom was afraid she would turn her into a toad or something. But now that I'm older, looking back, I think she just respected her that much. She was our grandmother on our father's side and, as little as we saw of her, it was more than we saw our father, which was basically never.

When my focus had strengthened and the distant rumble of thunder had moved far into the background, I opened my eyes and rested both palms over the bowl. With each breath in, I moved my hands clockwise; with each breath out, I moved my hands counter clockwise. Back and forth, forth and back, until I could feel the heat building between my palms and the surface of the water. I held onto the energy for as long as I could and then with an exhale, I clapped my hands and released it. The water rippled in the bowl as if I had dropped a stone into its center. When the ripples calmed, I closed my eyes once again.

"Absorb our angst
Remove all negativity,
Purify this space
Leaving peace to be."

I stood and carried the bowl to the kitchen counter so Karma wouldn't drink it.

"All right, boy." I turned off the lights and lit a few candles. "The place should be cleansed soon and hopefully you'll start to feel better." I was already feeling the knots in my shoulders loosen. Of course, the meditation aspect of the ritual helped. One of the nice things about being human, we can consciously try to control our thoughts.

I flipped on the oven light and checked on the treats. They were turning a nice sandy brown, almost done. Just then, I heard a low rumble in the apartment. I stood up and looked over the kitchen counter. Karma stood at the French doors, the fur up on his back, his ears forward, growling a warning.

"What is it, boy?" I crossed the living room and opened the doors. He stepped cautiously out onto the balcony and lowered his head to peer between the flower table and the iron railing, out into the park. I flicked off the balcony lights and tried to see what he found so threatening. Despite the distant promise of a storm, the sky was clear and chocked-full of stars. And then a shadow caught my eye. It stepped out from behind the banyan tree and stood still. Too still. Was it watching us? The hair raised on my arms. Karma jumped up on the railing and—for a brief, terrifying second—I thought he was going to jump. Instead, he gave two deep, warning barks. The shadow turned and ran back through the park. I put a comforting hand on Karma's head.

"It's all right." I moved my gaze from the disappearing shadow to the sky. Grandma Winters had taught us to ask for protection from the stars. She said they were celestial beings in a living universe. I wasn't sure if they could hear or not, but it couldn't hurt. I whispered a little appeal for them to watch over us and then smiled as one seemed to wink back at me.

"Come on, Karma." He followed me back inside and I locked the door. Whoever it was had been watching us. I was sure of it. Why though?

I kept the lights out, feeling safer in the candlelight. Karma seemed content to stretch out in front of the French doors, keeping watch. After I pulled the hot treats from the oven and wrapped them up, I grabbed a pillow from the bed and got comfortable on the couch. I woke up a few times through the night thinking about Mad Dog. His words kept coming back to me in ghostly sound bites. "It's my own fault." Those were his words. But what exactly did they mean?

TWENTY

Sylvia had noticed our customers enjoyed hanging out and chatting in the store so we decided to put a few wicker chairs by the front window, a table with a hot water dispenser and some bowls of assorted teas from Hooker Tea Company. This proved to be a big hit Monday morning.

Sarah Applebaum waited around while Sylvia groomed Lady Elizabeth, chatting with two of her friends who had stopped in to buy flower essence and make appointments for their own pampered pooches.

I wasn't trying to be nosey, but I heard them mention Frankie's name so I tuned in.

"It's by personal invitation only," Sarah was saying, blowing into her cup of tea. "I had a message last night. I'm sure you'll get a call today."

They were talking about the banquet. Frankie had decided it'd be too short notice to send mailed invitations; and, besides, people would feel all the more special being "personally" invited over the phone.

"Of course." The woman smoothed down her shiny black bob, gold bracelets clanging with the motion. "Where is she holding it?"

"The Vinoy Resort, poolside."

"I guess it will be updos, ladies," the tall, thin woman remarked. "The humidity will be murder on our hair."

"Don't be negative, Patrice. It'll be fine." Sarah frowned. "We haven't had a big event here in awhile. And lord knows I need something to look forward to."

"Of course, you poor thing. I'm being insensitive to your pending divorce." The tall woman rested a long hand on her shoulder. "Men." She made a noise in her throat that sounded like she was trying to dislodge a hairball. "Disgusting creatures. In your own bed, no less."

I polished the computer keys for the third time. I guess Sarah discovered her husband's blonde side dish. I was starting to feel bad about eavesdropping. Luckily the door bells jingled.

"Hi, Darwin."

It was Detective... I mean, Will. He brought the morning sunshine in with him, all warm and fresh, with the promise of a new beginning. He was wearing tan slacks and a blue silk tie that matched his eyes.

"Morning, Will." I mirrored his smile. It felt good to see him again. "What are you up to?"

"Gotta be in court today but wanted to see if I could pin you down for dinner Saturday night before you fill up your schedule."

The women behind him had gone silent. I guess all's fair in love and eavesdropping.

"Oh, well. You're too late." I know, that was bad. I just wanted to see how disappointed he would be.

"Oh." His smile dropped.

I couldn't keep it going. His disappointment affected me too much. "Actually, Frankie Maslow and I are putting on a charity event at the Vinoy Saturday night to benefit the homeless. And," I smiled up at him, "I was going to see if you wanted to be my..." uh oh. I hadn't really thought this out.

"Date?" His eyes flashed with new hope and familiar humor.

"Yes." There. Date. This would be a date.

"Hmmm." Now he was teasing me. Was I squirming? "Well, I suppose, since I won't be busy."

After he gave Karma a good scratch, and I gave him a time to meet me, he walked to the door.

"Ladies." He smiled as he left.

"Mmm mmm mmm, Miss Darwin," Sarah Applebaum craned her neck to watch him out the window. "That Detective Blake is one hunk of a man. I tried to set him up with my niece last year but he wasn't ready to date yet. How'd you manage to get him back in the dating pool?"

I opened my mouth and then closed it again. There were a few things that bothered me. One, why did it surprise her that he would want to date me? And two, why wasn't he ready to date yet?

"Just remember all men are dogs, dear, and you'll be fine," the tall woman said.

Youch, that chip on her shoulder must be heavy.

"Speakin' of dogs." The dark haired lady smiled and pointed toward the back of the boutique.

"Oh, hello, precious!" Sarah Applebaum got up and clapped her hands as Sylvia came down the aisle with a prancing Lady Elizabeth. "Don't you just look like a little princess?"

Thank heavens Sylvia saved me. If this is what I had to look forward to at the benefit, it was going to be a long night.

TWENTY-ONE

I don't know where she shops, but somehow Sylvia managed to scrounge me up a gorgeous vintage cocktail dress for the benefit which, as I admired it in the mirror, just happened to fit me like a glove. It was silver with lines of sparkly sequin accents, spaghetti straps and a deep v-line back... oh, and a silk lining so the whole thing didn't make my skin crawl. I would have to thank her a million more times because this was the one thing that had given me fits all week—worrying about what I was going to wear.

"Not too bad, eh, Karma?"

Karma eyed me from his position sprawled out on the bed. He didn't seem impressed. Of course, he was pouting because I was leaving him alone.

"Don't go giving me those big brown, sad eyes. This is for a good cause. For our friends." I pulled the bobby pins carefully out of my hair. Sylvia had taught me how to tame my hair with them so it now rested in soft waves across my forehead. I pinned it back at my left temple with a diamond barrette; threw on some mascara and some pink cream blush; and removed my mala bead bracelets and replaced them with a dainty silver watch. Done. That's about all the primping I could stand for one night. I checked the watch. I still had thirty minutes before Will would arrive to walk to the Vinoy together.

I descended the stairs and went to the kitchen counter, flipped open my laptop and typed in 'Frat Boys Inc.' Unspecified business, blab blah blah blah. Nothing. I had a sinking feeling I was going to have to step up my investigation to something more dangerous than internet searches. I had to get inside that townhouse.

***

As I stepped out into the balmy evening and closed the gate, Sylvia and Landon Stark walked toward me.

"Oh!" Sylvia—in a shimmery black dress, her hair in an elegant knot—hugged me tight. "*Você olha como um anjo!*" She held me at arm's length and smiled her approval. "You look like an angel."

"Thanks to you," I said. "And you look gorgeous as always." I adjusted the basket in my arm to shake Landon's hand. "Thanks for donating the tickets, Landon."

"Of course." He kissed my hand. He looked as slick as ever in a black tux, his hair and skin scrubbed to a shine.

"Oh," I turned to Sylvia, "I hope you don't mind, I added a free grooming certificate to the items in here." I patted the basket.

"No, no. It's a good idea."

"Wow."

We turned around and my face flushed. Will stood there, looking polished and perfect in a black tux. His eyes were raking my body, sending waves of heat rushing over me. I wiggled my toes around in my strappy heels trying to dispel some of the energy.

"Hi."

Sylvia gave a low laugh and whispered in my ear. "That is what we call smitten."

Will shook Landon's hand and said hello to Sylvia but his eyes quickly moved back to me. I wasn't sure what to do, suddenly. I felt too exposed, too self-conscious. Luckily, Sylvia saved me from a decision when she looped her arm in Landon's, threw one last grin my way and headed towards the Vinoy.

Will took the basket from me. "I'll carry that for you." Then offered me his arm. I slipped my arm through his; the contact sending a new ripple of energy up my arm that spidered out to the rest of my body. I sucked in a breath.

Will kept sneaking glances down at me. "You look amazing."

"Thank you. You're not so bad yourself." I smiled up at him. I felt like I could float, just from being this close to him, touching him, smelling that peculiar mixture of coconut and fresh rain that I associated with him now. Along with the sticky, summer evening air; the moonlight and promise of the night to come, I felt like I had stepped into a fairytale. Is this what it felt like to fall in love?

Whoa. Full stop. At that thought I tensed up. Okay, Darwin, what are you doing? Setting yourself up to get hurt, that's what. Stop it. Love means honesty. If you were honest with him about who you are, he'd leave. Don't ruin everything. This had to stay casual. A dinner once in awhile. That's all.

I blinked back warm tears. I had never felt this vulnerable before. I was on an emotional roller coaster that was threatening to derail. He seemed to sense my struggle.

"You okay?" He pulled me closer into him.

"Yeah." I wiped beneath my eye, using my finger as a dam for the tears. "A bug flew in my eye is all." I leaned into him, void of will power. His presence was like a wall, a shield between me and the world. I felt... safe. I was in serious trouble.

***

We made our way through the main hall of the renaissance styled Vinoy Resort, down a set of tiled stairs, then across an outdoor patio and up a second set of stairs. At the top, the pool sparkled beneath a row of palms. The lawn chairs had been removed. Positioned around the pool were small tables wrapped in white, silk cloth. Live orchids served as centerpieces.

Servers in white balanced silver trays full of hors d'oeuvres and champagne flutes. A man in a white tux sat stroking a piano to our left. I spotted Frankie greeting the guests.

"Darwin!" She rushed over in her three inch gold heels, which matched her gold dress designed like a large bow. "Oh, isn't it just a perfect evening."

"Perfect, yes. And you're looking very festive." We air kissed. "Where should I put the basket?"

"Hello, glad you all could make it." She gave Sylvia, Will and Landon a quick hug, then pointed to the right side of the pool. "The auction table is over there. I'll catch up with you in a bit. Grab a glass of champagne."

We moved closer to the pool. Hundreds of tea lights burned, floating on the surface, a waterfall, like a glistening sheet of rain made up the back wall. It made me miss my youngest sister, Mallory. Fire was her thing. We were complete opposites, fire and water. Together, our magick was strong.

Will and Landon plucked two glasses each from a tray and we all held up the flutes.

"A toast," Will said. "To a successful benefit and to a magical evening."

His eyes held mine over the clinking glasses. Why did he use the word "magical"? Are my thoughts floating through the ether into his mind? I swallowed the champagne in two mouthfuls and grabbed another flute.

"And to good champagne," Sylvia added, clinking my new glass with a wink. "*Pôr-se.*" Slipping her arm around my waist, she whispered, "Relax. Enjoy." She smelled like cedar and cloves.

Relax. Enjoy. Okay, I could do that. I willed my shoulders to unknot and took a deep breath.

"Hello, gals!" Sarah Applebaum and company sauntered up to us in all their glittered, powdered, sprayed and painted glory.

"Alô, ladies." Sylvia raised her glass to them.

"Hi, Mrs. Applebaum." I introduced myself to her friends. "Nice to see you again."

"And you, detective," Sarah Applebaum poked Will's chest with a long red nail, her eyes narrowing. "Back in the dating world and you didn't call my niece. She's not going to be happy to hear that."

"My loss, I'm sure."

I tried to keep the smile plastered on my face, but heavens that was rude. Glancing at Will, he didn't seem too pleased with her little admonishment, either. He slipped his hand into mine.

"If you ladies will excuse me, I'm going to dance with my lovely date."

He led me near the piano, took the glass from my hand and pulled me into his arms. "I'm so sorry you had to be there for that."

"No biggie," I managed to push out on breath that was becoming more and more precious. My whole body was pressed into his. I could feel the solidness of his chest under the crisp tux lapels;

feel the heat warming my low back where his hand rested. I'd had dance lessons but this was my first time being in the arms of a man that lit me on fire from the inside out. I was starting to be a believer in spontaneous combustion.

As he rested his cheek on top of my head, and we swayed in slow motion under the stars, there were so many things I wanted to ask—to know—about him. But I had no right to ask. I had no right to try to enter this man's world when I had no intention of being a part of it. An ache of loss and longing bloomed in my chest, and I hadn't even lost anything yet.

"You smell like flowers," he whispered into my hair, breathing me in like I was, in fact, a flower.

I squeezed my eyes closed and my resolve faltered. All right. One question. It would be all right to ask just one question.

"Will?"

"Hm?"

"What happened? I mean, why weren't you dating?"

He cleared his throat. "I was married. We went to college together, married after graduation, made it about five years then... then she left me for a German plastic surgeon; left the country. Took our cat."

I braced myself for the waves of anger, regret or sadness that usually accompany a confession like that. They came but were more like soft echoes from the past. That was a good thing. "How long has it been?"

"Six years this August."

I stopped swaying and pulled away from him. "You haven't dated in six years?"

"Wow." He pressed his wrist against my forehead. "You're burning up. Your face is flushed. Are you feeling okay?"

"I'm fine." Hot, yeah. His fault. "Are you changing the subject?"

"No," he laughed. "Yes. It's been six years. That surprises you?"

"Well, yeah." It stunned me, actually. This town was packed with gorgeous, successful women with the money and drive to stay gorgeous and successful. "What'd you do, hide under a rock?"

"No." He entangled our fingers. "I just hadn't met anyone I was interested in."

"Oh, and then I come along and spill tea all over you and you said, "Yep here's the girl I've been waitin' for." I laughed... until I looked up and he had that intensity burning in his eyes again.

"Exactly," he whispered, lowering his mouth to mine. I froze. It was a soft brush of lips, an entanglement of emotions, expectations. His hand cupped the back of my neck and he touched his lips to mine, lightly at first and then—as the intensity and hunger of his kiss grew—I had to close my eyes and lean against him so I didn't fall over. Stars burst behind my eyes. His mouth was hot and tasted like champagne. His energy was fierce and my own mouth felt like a furnace. He pulled back slowly from the kiss, his eyes closed.

We were still only an inch away when we made eye contact again. I was burning up, wiggling my toes, feeling light headed and like I had just found the notorious "cloud nine."

"So," I whispered, "she took the cat?"

A smile. Heavens, I was growing fond of that smile.

"I can get another cat." He leaned in and kissed me again.

"This is a hotel, you know. You two can get a room." Sylvia and Landon had joined us in dancing, along with a few other couples. Her dark eyes were so full of humor as she swayed close by, they actually glowed.

I hid my face in Will's tux and felt the deep rumble of his laughter.

He kissed the top of my head. "Let's go get you a drink to cool off." He took my hand. "Are you sure you're feeling okay?"

"Yeah." I gave him a dopey smile. Couldn't help it, it was a silly question. I hadn't felt this good... well, ever.

We swiped two glasses of champagne off a tray and went to join Frankie, who was laughing with a small group of women, each holding plates full of tiny, rolled and decorated appetizers. I was surprised to see how crowded the space around the pool had become while I was... preoccupied. Was the whole city of St. Pete here?

"Oh, Darwin, come here, sugar," Frankie said. I felt Will's reluctance to let go of my hand and smiled to myself. "I want to introduce you to my friend and real estate agent, Betsy Mills."

"Nice to meet you." I shook her hand.

"Betsy has three standard poodles, one in each color! I told her she must come visit your new pet boutique." Frankie winked at me and her eyelashes stuck together for a second. She pulled at them with her thumb and forefinger—a large ruby bracelet sliding down her freckled arm—then continued. "And when you're ready to buy property here, Betsy's your gal. She's got the inside scoop on all the deals."

I was quite happy in the Beach Drive townhouse, but I thanked her anyway. I glanced over at Will. He had gotten himself cornered by two women who kept touching his arms as they chatted. His eyes were still on me. I gave him a little wave and he mouthed "help." I held my glass up with a grin and then took a sip of the bubbly.

"So, go on, Jo Anne," the lady with spiky red hair and a black sequined gown said, as she popped an appetizer without messing up her perfectly lined and colored lips. How do women do that?

"So, they don't want me to do cardio for another week, but I'm just a little sore now."

"Can I feel 'em?" the redhead asked.

"Sure."

I about dropped my glass when she reached over and squeezed Jo Anne's breast.

"They do feel natural." She nodded. "I think it's good you didn't go too big."

I snapped my mouth shut and nodded in agreement, trying not to act like the obviously sheltered-from-plastic-surgery-etiquette woman that I was. Mental note: it's fine to ask someone to feel their new boobs.

Frankie moved closer to whisper to me. "We'll wait about an hour to start the auction. Let everyone relax and drink first. Bids will be higher."

"You did a really great job putting this together on such short notice, Frankie. How did you ever get them to close off the whole pool for us?"

She winked. "I called in a favor."

"Well, I hope the auction will cover renting this place and the food. It must have cost a fortune."

"Oh, believe me. These women will be generous. We get their money, they get to feel good about themselves. It's a win win."

Just then, gasps began around us. I whirled around to where some of the women were staring, clutching their necklines, chins dropped in stunned silence. The piano fell silent and a hush made its way toward us in a wave from the stairs.

"Ah, no," Frankie groaned.

TWENTY-TWO

He stumbled toward us, the dark kid from Pirate City, his arm wrapped around his stomach. A red bandana circled his forehead and he wore a pair of dirty jeans. No shoes, no shirt. As everyone else moved back, Frankie and I stepped out of the crowd. I looked from the kid to Frankie. She was frowning, her mouth working back and forth. Trying to figure out how to handle this, I'm sure. The kid's breathing came in heavy gulps. As he fell toward us, I could see angry, fresh needle marks on his arms.

I looked around at the knots of people, staring and beginning to whisper. Will had moved closer to Frankie, his hands on his hips— waiting.

"Junior," Frankie said, as he finally stood in front of her, wobbling and sweating. "I'm going to get Vick to take you out of here."

"I need a doctor," he breathed out.

"You need rehab." She bent down to look into his eyes.

"Well, I'm calling the police," the woman with newly minted boobs spoke up.

"Yeah, Frankie, don't get too close, he might have a gun or somethin'."

"He's stoned out of his mind."

"Get him out of here!"

"Hey!" Junior yelled, spit flying at their glittering costumes with his words. "You bitches shut up. What do you have to complain about? You don't know what problems are! Just shut up!"

All right, this was getting out of hand. I either had just enough of everyone's crap or just enough champagne, but it was my turn to speak up.

"Hey, Junior." He turned and focused his anger and pain on me. I stood my ground. "Just because people have money doesn't mean they don't have problems. Betrayal, addictions and pain aren't reserved for the poor."

"You tell him!" Someone yelled.

I whirled around. "And y'all should be ashamed of yourselves. Stop staring at him like he's some zoo animal. This is a human being and the very reason that we are all here tonight. For him." I pointed at Junior. "Y'all need to stop judging each other."

Just then there was a splash, then screaming and chaos. Junior had fallen into the pool.

Will threw off his tux jacket and jumped in the pool after him. Some of the tea light candles went out, some sank.

"Now you can call an ambulance," I told the redhead.

***

Will kneeled on the Mexican tiled patio, chlorine water dripping from him, pumping Junior's chest until he rolled over and threw up water. I grabbed some cloth napkins, folded them up and placed them under Junior's head to cushion it from the tile. His body was shaking pretty badly and his eyes weren't focusing on anything in particular.

"Is he gonna be all right?" I asked Will, who was untucking his white dress shirt and wringing it out at the bottom. I caught a glimpse of smooth skin over taut muscle and turned away. The heat crawled up my neck anyway.

"Don't know. Ambulance should be here soon, though." We could hear the sirens getting closer.

"I've got a car here." Vick leaned over us, assessing Junior. "I can take him to the hospital."

I glanced up at Vick. Frankie was holding onto his arm, her eyes wide. What in the world does she see in him? "That's kind of you, but sounds like the paramedics are here."

Sure enough, a few moments later, two paramedics were carrying a stretcher on wheels up the stairs and then toward us.

As they assessed Junior and put him on the stretcher, Will relayed the events in the typical detailed cop fashion.

"All right, everyone." Frankie clapped her hands after the drama was over and Junior was on his way to the hospital. "I'm glad you got to see that." Everyone quietly turned to her. "That poor boy is a victim. He's a victim of a society that doesn't take care of its own people. Darwin's right. We all treat our pets better than we treat each other." Er, I didn't say that. But, she had a point. "If that boy was perfect—not addicted to drugs, had a safe place to live and food to eat... then he wouldn't need us, right?" A few people murmured. "I said... right?!"

"Right!" a chorus of voices answered.

"That's right. He needs us. That's why we are here tonight. So, let's get this auction started and help that poor boy and the others that need us!"

As everyone made their way over to the table of items to be auctioned off, Will turned to me.

"I really hate to do this, but I'm going to have to cut out early." He motioned to his soaked clothes and frowned. Then he slipped his hands in mine with a slight grin. "You could come with me?"

"To your house and watch you strip off a newly ruined tux?" I laughed, though the image caused unfamiliar flutterings in my stomach. "I don't think I'm ready for that kind of trouble."

"Fair enough." He leaned in and kissed me softly. I could taste the chlorine but I didn't care. I sighed. He groaned. "When can I see you again?"

Oh heavens. I was getting in so over my head here. Losing control. Was that a bad thing? There was no stop button on this crazy ride and I was already dizzy from the spin. "You know where to find me." I smiled, shook my head and then went to find Sylvia. It took all my self control not to look back.

She had found a lounge chair and was sitting with Landon, watching the auction. Her black heels had been discarded below the chair and Landon had his jacket off. They looked so comfortable—with themselves, with each other. I was envious.

"Ah, there you are," she said, as I approached and plopped down in the chair next to her. "Your Romeo has left you?"

What was the saying? The cat who ate the canary? Yeah, she was smiling at me like that.

"Alas, yes," I sighed for added drama. "He had to go peel off some wet clothes after his heroics in the pool." I looked at her sharply. "And no comment about him undressing."

Landon laughed at that and stood. "I'll get you ladies a refill and leave you to your girl talk." He kissed Sylvia's cheek and she whispered something in his ear that made him feign shock. He winked at me before heading off. I still couldn't decide if I trusted him or not.

"So?" Sylvia turned her full attention to me.

I groaned in frustration. "Yes. He's amazing. He's smart and funny and has those incredible blue eyes and that smile that makes my heart tumble and... and..." I threw up my hands.

"And he is crazy about you, too. Good." She eyed me. "What is problem?"

"I don't know what to do with it all. These new feelings and I don't know how I'm supposed to be around him. Am I letting things move too fast? I mean, I feel like I'm on a roller coaster." And I can't let him get too close. I can't let him know about the parts of me that would make him run screaming in the other direction. Really, I couldn't let Sylvia in on those parts of me either. I suddenly felt tired, spent and alone. "I'm sorry. I'm just overwhelmed."

"Darwin, you just be you. Just Darwin. Everything else will be what it is, too."

I smiled. "So, things are going good with your magician, I see."

"And speak of the devil." Her eyes lit up as Landon returned with three fresh glasses.

Okay, I wasn't the only one on the roller coaster. I didn't feel so lonely after all.

***

By eleven o'clock, the auction had ended and we had all made the trip from tipsy to tired. I strolled over to say good night to Frankie; strappy heels in hand, the warm night air like a comforting blanket around me.

"So, a success?" I hugged her. She looked as tired as I felt. Her hair had frizzed at the edges from the humidity and her makeup had melted. But she did look happy.

"Absolutely, sugar. Guilt does wonders on the conscience. We'll have to get together with my accountant this week and figure out how much we have to spend and what the camp needs."

"Sounds great. Any updates on Junior's condition?"

"Well, I called and they're keeping him overnight. He's stable, though. Me and Vick are gonna go see him first thing in the morning."

I glanced at Vick. All I could picture was his hands around Maddy's neck. I swallowed the distaste that rose up in my throat but held his eye contact. "That's very kind of you to care." Then I turned to Frankie. "Have you been able to talk to Maddy yet? Find out why she left you so abruptly?"

"She's still not taking my calls," she sighed. "It's breakin' my heart."

"That's so strange. Don't you think, Vick?" I raised an eyebrow at him. "Since her and Frankie were so close? Any ideas?"

I thought I detected a sharpening of his attention on me, like he had suddenly sat up and looked at me for the first time. His eyes narrowed. "No. None."

"Well, I'm sure you'll get to the bottom of it eventually, Frankie," I said, still staring at Vick. I smiled. He didn't. "Speaking of that. Maybe when y'all visit Junior tomorrow, you could get to the bottom of his injuries. See if you can get him to tell you who's beating him up. He trusts you, Frankie. Maybe he'll talk to you."

"He's a homeless junkie," Vick scoffed. "He's hurtin' himself."

"Well, we can certainly talk to him." Frankie shot Vick an annoyed look. "Don't forget where I came from."

"Course not. I'm just sayin', he's probably into more stuff than just drugs."

"And I'm just sayin' that Mad Dog had the same injuries and he wasn't into drugs."

"Mad Dog?"

"Yeah, the homeless guy who committed suicide at Mirror Lake a few weeks back. Only..." Frankie looked from me to Vick. "Darwin doesn't believe it was suicide. She thinks somebody killed him."

"That so?" Vick said. He looked me up and down. "You knew him?"

"Yes. He was my friend." I said friend with extra emphasis because I knew where his slimy mind would go.

His thin mouth spread into an amused grin. Reminded me of a snake. I waited for a little forked tongue to shoot out. But, instead, I got a shot of his attempt at humor.

"Friends don't let friends drink and swim."

Okay, it was time to go. This guy was really ticking me off. I turned my shoulder toward him and said good night to Frankie.

I heard them begin to argue as I walked away.

TWENTY-THREE

Not one for being patient, I decided the next night, Sunday, would be as good a night as any to break into the town house. Or, at least do some serious spying. Again, the hardest part was deciding what to wear. I mean, I couldn't go strolling down the street in all black... or could I?

I settled on black yoga pants and a dark purple t-shirt. Oh, and an olive green knitted cap to hide my hair, which glowed the same color as moonlight in the dark.

"What?" I rested my hands on my hips and stared back at Karma. "You worried, big guy?"

Kneeling down in front of the bed where his paws and chin hung off, I slid my hands underneath his floppy ears. "You're such a sensitive soul, aren't you? Don't worry about me. I'll be careful. A promise is a promise, right?" He lifted his head and licked my forearm. I wiped it on my shirt. "Thanks. Now, you promise to go easy on the pillow drool. Stay on the towel. That's an order." I rubbed his head one last time and stood up. Time to go.

It took longer to get there since I opted to walk instead of worrying about a bike. I didn't realize how vulnerable I would feel walking in the dark, especially without Karma by my side. No fast getaways tonight.

I lingered in front of the house, trying to spot any movement. The sunroom in front was all windows and dark inside. Glancing up and down the sidewalk, I decided my best bet would be the back door. Hurrying between the houses, where a path had been worn in the grass, I circled around back and pressed myself against the house, praying no one was home because the drum beat in my chest would surely give me away.

Muffled music boomed from the house next door, competing with the nasal calls of tree frogs and chirping crickets, but all seemed quiet inside. Okay, deep breath…. it's now or never.

I crept through the overgrown weeds to the brown door above cement steps and peered through the window into the kitchen. No signs of life. Unfolding the penknife on my keychain, I shoved it between the crack and door frame. After a bit of clumsy jiggling, the door clicked open. Well, what do you know, it worked! Thank you, internet.

I tiptoed in and shut the door behind me. Only then did it hit me the place could have had an alarm. The blood drained to my toes and I listened—silence except the sound of the refrigerator running. Whew. Got lucky, but I'd have to be more careful. This breaking and entering stuff was nerve-wracking. I stood still until my breathing was normal enough to hear movement above the sound of my own fear. The plan was in and out. Find something, anything to figure out who lived here and why Mad Dog had been here that night.

I shined a pen light around the kitchen. The counter between the fridge and stove was packed with liquor bottles. I ventured in and opened the drawers. Empty. I opened the fridge. Two cases of beer, one half empty. So, this place probably wasn't being used as a home. What then? A bar? Well, the name Frat Boys, Inc. was starting to make sense.

I moved into the next room and hugged the wall so I wouldn't run into anything, making it to the first window. Heavy material hung under the curtain. Same with the second window. Slowly, as my eyes adjusted, I could see a few shapes to my left. I swept the pen light in that direction. Just then I heard a car door shut outside. I flicked the light off and stood frozen, listening. Was that voices? If they came in the front door, I could probably make it back out the kitchen door. What would I say if they caught me? Sorry, wrong house? My mind was scrambling as fast as my heart.

A car started. Drove away. I released the breath I had been holding. Okay, Darwin. Hurry. I moved toward the shapes, wishing I had brought a bigger flash light. Some kind of chest sat against the wall. I tried to open it. Locked. Next to it sat a big silver case, also locked. A tripod stood next to that. Getting frustrated, I crossed the empty room—the wood floor squeaking under my steps—and into the first bedroom. Nothing of interest, just some barbells and weights stacked to one side. The next room had a desk. I slipped in and sat down in front of the monitor. A computer, yes! Oh please be on. I wiggled the mouse and the screen lit up. My heart sank. Password required. I shuffled around in the desk, but it was empty. Someone was being very careful.

The third and final room had a blow up mattress and stacks of sheets, towels and pillows. Weird. Somewhere for people to sleep off all that alcohol, maybe?

Time to get out of there. I was really starting to feel like I was pushing my luck.

I hurried back out through the kitchen door—not realizing how cranked up the air conditioner had been in there until the steamy night air hit me—back between the houses and crossed the street. That's when the car pulled up.

I hopped behind a palm tree jutting up from the sidewalk. The little black sports car stayed running but the headlights flicked off. Someone, a female, stepped out of the passenger side. I peered out, hoping the driver behind the tinted glass wouldn't spot me.

As I watched the woman walk up the sidewalk and enter the house, I wracked my brain. She looked familiar. Where had I seen her before? She was in and out in less than a minute and, as she walked back to the car, the moonlight was enough for me to see her face. It wasn't a woman, it was a girl—one of the twins who worked with Landon Stark.

As I tried to make myself the size and shape of the palm tree, I chewed on this new piece of the puzzle. Did this mean that Landon owned the townhouse? That he had something to do with Mad Dog's death? Oh heavens, I hoped that wasn't true. That would break Sylvia's heart.

TWENTY-FOUR

It was a stormy Wednesday afternoon before I saw Will again. He strolled through the door of the boutique, shaking off a black umbrella and looking very serious in his slacks and detective shield.

"Hi." I managed. All kinds of things swirled around inside me. Things I didn't know how to deal with. Guilt for one—I had promised him no more dangerous investigating. And the battle to get close to him—something that couldn't happen no matter how much my heart was begging for it.

"You avoiding me?" His voice was so tender. His smile, too.

Yes. Now I felt guilty about that, too. "No, of course not."

"I've left you about a dozen messages. Gives a guy a complex when a girl doesn't call back, you know." He reached out and stroked my hand, which was resting on the counter. "I've missed you."

"I missed you, too." My shoulders slumped. Was I even up for this battle? Grandma Winters had prepared us girls for lots of other dangers but no one bothered to tell us what to do to keep from losing our hearts. "Just going through some stuff. You know, personal stuff I have to work out." That was pretty close to the truth. I could live with myself for that excuse.

"Can you get away for lunch?" I was about to say no, but then he added: "I've got some information for you. The autopsy report is back."

Mad Dog's autopsy report? My heart did a flip flop. I couldn't say no to that.

"Let me see if Sylvia's almost done with the Yorkie. Be right back."

We stepped out into the downpour ten minutes later, his arm around my shoulders, his umbrella over our heads. Safe against him, with the scent of the rain, was almost happiness overload. I kept reminding myself this had to be temporary—which made it all the sweeter and more painful.

We opted for a short sprint to the Parkshore Grill and still arrived with soaked feet and arms. The hostess led us to one of their comfy dark oak booths in the corner. The perfect seat for watching the rain and lightning show out of the double glass doors. I felt myself relaxing in the dim atmosphere with the smell of fried seafood wafting from the kitchen.

We ordered some hot seafood chowder to warm us up. "So," Shivering, I wiped off my arms with the cloth napkin. "What did the autopsy report say?"

Will reached across the table and covered my wrists with one of his large hands, his thumb fidgeting with my mala beads. Long pulses of warm energy slid up my arms. Oh heavens, the rain was turning up the intensity. I suddenly didn't need the soup. "It said that you were right. The tox screen showed no alcohol or drugs in his system." He stopped, letting that sink in.

I was right? I mean, I had felt I was right but it was so different from knowing for sure. The relief was like bags of sand being lifted off my chest. Mad Dog hadn't fallen off the wagon. He had been faithful to himself and to Karma. He had kept his promise. And died anyway. Why?

I waited until the waiter filled our water glasses before I asked the big question.

"And the cause of death?"

"Was not drowning." Will's eyes crinkled with compassion, though his tone of voice revealed pure frustration. "There was no water in his lungs. He was deceased before he hit the lake."

"Which... which means that someone had to have put him in the lake, right? I mean, if he was already gone, he couldn't have got in there by himself."

"Seems to be the logical conclusion, yes."

"So, how did he die?"

"It was a brain hemorrhage."

"And that's caused by?"

"Most likely head trauma. Mr. Fowler also had a hairline fracture to his skull. And," he was watching me closely, making sure I still wanted him to go on. "And two broken ribs that were healing, but recent."

I moved my hands up to cover my mouth. I knew it. "I should have done something. I knew he was getting hurt and I didn't do anything." Warm tears spilled down my cheeks. Will reached across and wiped at them with his thumb.

"I won't let you blame yourself, Darwin. Mr. Fowler was a grown man. He made his own decisions. He could have come to the police if he wanted to."

I shook my head. "Why didn't he want to?"

"I don't know, but look," he held my gaze. "You should feel better. Something is being done now. His case will be treated as a homicide and investigated. That's what you wanted, right?"

Yeah, that did make me feel a little better. It wouldn't bring him back but at least I wouldn't be the only one trying to figure out what happened that night.

"So, what about the suicide note?"

He sighed. "I really shouldn't be discussing the investigation any further with you."

The waiter brought our soup. "Thank you."

He stared at me through the steam, a round of thunder shaking the glass doors. "That will be the first thing I check into. I'll talk to the person at Pirate City who turned over the note and try to figure out why someone would forge it."

I stuck a spoon in my soup and stirred it. "Well, we know why. To try and cover up his murder." I wanted to ask him who at Pirate City had given them the note, but I knew he wouldn't tell me.

There were things I could tell him: about the townhouse and Landon's assistants having access to it; about Vick hurting Maddy; about Karma's reaction to the two policemen. But, I wasn't sure what any of it meant. And besides, I couldn't tell him without telling him *how* I knew these things.

"There's something else I thought you might want to know." He pulled a card from his pocket and slid it across the table to me.

I looked at the card. On it was written: Mariah 1/26/03

"What's this?"

"It was a tattoo on his right arm. A heart. You want to find his next of kin? Give him a proper place of rest? He probably had a daughter. I'd start looking on the internet for a Mariah Fowler."

A daughter? Oh my heavens. A tiny spark, like a firecracker, burst in my chest. "Thank you, Will." 2003? She would be what? Eight years old? He said he didn't have any family, though. Why wouldn't he tell me about a daughter?

TWENTY-FIVE

Frankie borrowed Vick's Ford pickup Saturday morning and, as we drove it down the street, loaded with items purchased with some of the benefit money, we could see the gang waiting for us. Frankie honked the horn.

We waved and slid out of the truck as everyone gathered around.

"All right, don't just stand around with your mouths open. Start hauling stuff out." Frankie laughed and lowered the gate. "Get the bikes out first. They're laying on top of the stove."

"Whoa! Bikes!" The pirate boy said.

"Those are not to sell; they're to get to jobs. Got me?" Frankie gave him a stern look.

"Yes, ma'am."

I waved at G, who stood in the back, cradling his box and singing, "We Wish You a Merry Christmas." Darn. In all the excitement, I forgot his cookies.

"Here, Pops." Frankie pointed inside the truck. "That box right there is heavy."

"Got it, Mama Maslow." Pops winked at her and pulled the box free.

"Minnie, you can get that one. It's just t-shirts."

They all worked together, pulling stuff out of the back and disappearing with it down the path and into the woods. I could hear the lightness in the voices echoing back toward us.

As Mac stood in the back, sliding the new tents and fresh water forward, I spotted a police cruiser coming down the road.

"Hey, Frankie." I nodded behind her. "Company."

She turned, mumbled something under her breath and then stepped out in the road to greet them. I was glad I had decided against bringing Karma today.

This time, I could see the driver. He was older and taller than the other officer—Officer Cruz. Frankie's hands were on her hips as she talked to him. She looked like she might be getting irritated. I walked over to see if I could help.

"Hello, officers." I put on my friendliest smile and glanced at Frankie. Yeah, her face looked like a tomato. "Something we can do for y'all this morning?"

"Oh, hey, the cookie lady." Officer Cruz leaned forward and smirked at me. "Well, I guess between you and Frankie, Pirate City is a thriving community."

Sarcasm is one of my least favorite things in this world. It makes me very sugary. "Just doing what any human being would do, Officer Cruz."

Frankie had her arms crossed now. "Hey, at least they're out of sight. That's what you want, right? No complaints from the rich folks downtown."

I glanced behind us. Pops and Mac were standing there watching the exchange now, looking worried. Everyone else had disappeared.

"What, you mean, rich people like you?" The older officer laughed. "That's a good one, Frankie."

"Oh, by the way," I put a steadying hand on Frankie's arm as she opened her mouth. "Did y'all know that Harold Barber was at Pirate City last week with a gun? He robbed and assaulted them."

"Robbed them?" Officer Cruz said. "Really? Well, no one filed a police report."

The older officer just kept staring at me with those steel eyes, smiling. No empathy there. His nametag was visible now: Officer Hutchins. I decided to pull my trump card.

"Well, if y'all could just keep your eye out for him. I mean, after all, there is a murderer running loose."

"A murderer?" Officer Hutchins gave off a healthy dose of indifference.

"Yeah. The person responsible for Mad Dog's death."

"The suicide?" Officer Hutchins blew out a little laugh.

"Oh, you haven't heard? Turns out there was no alcohol in his system and he didn't drown." I lowered my voice. "He died from blunt force trauma to the head."

In the span of silence that followed, I paid close attention to every twitch and emotion around the officers. There wasn't much: no guilt, no sadness. Nothing.

"Well, that's too bad." Officer Hutchins shrugged at Frankie and smiled. "See ya around, Maslow."

We watched them navigate the circle. Officer Cruz flicked a hand out the window as they drove back by us.

"Jerks." Frankie glanced at me. "Hey, is that true? About Mad Dog?"

"Yeah, unfortunately. Will got the autopsy report back. Someone definitely killed him and threw him in the lake."

"Christ on a cross." She shook her head.

"You all right?" Mac asked.

"Yeah, fine. They're just playing cop." Frankie said, still distracted. "Hey, I gotta talk to Minnie for a sec. You can wait in the truck if you want."

"Sure." I closed the truck gate. "Hey, Mac, can I talk to you for a sec?"

As Frankie moved into the woods, Mac walked over. "What's up?"

"The detective ask you about the suicide note yet? You know, the one found in the camp that Mad Dog supposedly wrote?"

Mac's face darkened.

"Come on, Mac. We both know he was killed. The note was a fake. Now the police know it, too."

"I know." He rubbed at a dirty forehead. "So, let them figure it out." He turned and walked away from me, his head low.

Sighing, I slipped back into the truck, started it and flipped on the air conditioner. My feet pushed at some papers lying on the floor mat. I picked them up and sorted through them. Receipts for repair work, a computer printout of directions. Nothing interesting. Glancing back down the path, I popped open the glove box. Ford books, some empty CD cases, more receipts for tires, gas, etc. Wait... what's this? I pulled out a pink envelope that was shoved between the books. There was a card inside. I slipped it out quickly. On the front was a single rose in gold glitter. The inside had two words scrolled across in more glitter: I'm sorry

At the top, someone had written: Dear Maddy

I shoved the card back into the glove box and closed it just as Frankie reappeared from the woods.

Had to be from Vick, right? Was he sorry for choking her? Why hadn't he given her the card? Maybe she wasn't speaking to him, either.

TWENTY-SIX

In between chatting with customers, ringing up sales and unpacking the new delivery on Monday, I spent the day on the internet trying to find Mariah Fowler, born on January 26th 2003. So far, my search took me to Myspace, find-a-grave, a geology forum and characteristics of a Capricorn. This was going to be harder than I thought.

Capricorn. Heavens. Willow, my middle sister, was a Capricorn. Her birthdays had always been full of delicious wintery themes, angel food coconut cake and homemade ice-cream. Would she even take my call this time around? Maybe I should go back for a visit, try to help them understand.

I sighed. Focus on one issue at a time, Darwin.

Sylvia appeared from the back with her white lab coat still pulled on over her snazzy lavender dress. I'd put money on the fact that she's the only woman around grooming dogs in designer clothes and heels. "Kat is still drying. Mrs. Berry is not here to pick her up yet?"

"Nope. Not yet." I clicked on one of the Myspace links. Maybe her mom had an account and mentioned her.

"Kat was extra nervous today, didn't want her feet handled. You might want to sell Mrs. Berry some flower essence."

"Okay." I smiled to myself. Sylvia had come a long way in accepting the flower essence.

"You are still looking for the little girl?"

"Yeah."

"Maybe she should not know her father has died."

I peered up into Sylvia's concerned eyes. "I know. I'm not bringing her good news. But, imagine when she's grown up and wonders why her father abandoned her? Wouldn't that be harder to live with?"

"Ah, yes. Maybe." The bells jingled as Mrs. Berry entered with a cheery wave.

Sylvia patted my arm. "I will pray you find her." Then took Mrs. Berry in the back to get Kat.

This one looked promising. It was a Tampa Daily News article about a 4H program. It mentioned a Mariah Fowler, though no age. 4H was for kids, right? She had to be young. It would make sense that if Mad Dog had a daughter, he would stick pretty close to where she lived when he came back from the war. Why didn't he go back to her? No use speculating on that question. There could be all kinds of issues with her mother. I opened up a new tab and searched the Tampa white pages for Fowler. My heart sank. There were five pages of them. I might have to solicit some help from my friends on this one— split up the list. It was a long shot, but what else could I do?

When Mrs. Berry left with Kat—and a bottle of aspen and cherry plum mixture—Sylvia smacked a hand on the counter. "You need a night to relax! We will have dinner at Landon's show tonight, some drinks, some laughs. Deal?"

I was about to say no, I'd rather spend the evening calling strangers named "Fowler" out of the phone book, but then I remembered Landon's assistant going into the townhouse. Maybe I could talk to the girls, do some digging. I put on my best excited face.

"Okay. Deal."

Sylvia blinked and her shoulders relaxed. "Well. Okay."

I think she was expecting a fight. This made me smile. She was turning out to be a good friend. My first real girlfriend outside my family. The trouble was, she didn't really know me. How much would it damage our friendship if she did know everything? And how much was I damaging it by keeping things from her?

"Thanks, Sylvia."

She nodded, tilting her head. "Hey, you invite Will, too?"

"Oh, I don't know."

"Listen," her hand went to her hip, "you have nothing to be scared of with him. He's a good guy."

Yeah, but am I good for him? It would be nice to see him again. "All right."

Turns out Will had to work but he did sound happy that I finally called him. Guess that was worth something.

***

So, Sylvia and I sat at the front table again, watching the spectacular show Landon put on. We really tried to figure out how he did some of his tricks and I was beginning to think Frankie may have been on to something. Maybe he did use real magic. He still seemed dark and secretive to me but were my suspicions fueled by his assistants showing up at the townhouse? Or maybe he just reminded me of my father—the most dark and secretive man in the world.

I shrugged off that thought with a shiver as Sylvia leaned in to whisper something to me.

By the time the show was over and Landon and Mage joined us at the table, I was full and relaxed. Sylvia had kept the table full of appetizers and our glasses full of a cold, white wine.

"Great show as always, Landon." I leaned over and stroked Mage's head. No zap. His dark eyes squinted in pleasure at the attention. "Though, I think Mage here stole the show with that fire trick."

"Oh!" Sylvia rested her hand on her chest. "That was very dangerous, no?"

"I wouldn't put Mage in danger." Landon took a seat and smiled at Sylvia. "You, on the other hand, I think you would enjoy the danger."

Sylvia gave a deep little laugh as they kissed.

I eyed Landon. Was he capable of being involved in Mad Dog's death? "Speaking of danger, Landon, have your assistants ever gotten hurt? They do some amazing tricks up there themselves?"

"Only once. Ah, speak of the devils." Landon waved the girls over as they exited the back stage, dressed in their street cloths. "Tammy, Tonya, this is my friend Darwin."

"Nice to meet you," I shook their hands. They looked similar but not identical. Tammy's face was rounder, her eyes a deeper blue than her sister's.

"Darwin was asking if you girls have ever gotten hurt during a show. Go on, Tonya, I know how much you love to tell that story."

Tonya gave him a little smirk. "Well, last year, we had this really awesome tank trick. Where Tammy got in the tank, I raised a curtain, then after a minute, me and Landon acted like we forgot about her. We were trying out some comedy."

Tammy jumped in. "What was supposed to happen was when Tonya raised the curtain, I would get out and would be sitting on top of the tank when the curtain finally dropped. But, my dear sister here thought it would be funny to really lock me in. I almost drowned."

Tonya laughed. "Oh, come on, are you still sore about that? I told you, I wouldn't have let you drown."

Landon winked at Tonya, "Well, *I* wouldn't have let you drown. The jury's still out on your sister."

"Ha ha, Mr. Comedian." Tonya crossed her arms. "Stick to magic. Anyways, we gotta split. Nice to meet you, Darwin."

"Charmed." I watched them leave together. I couldn't imagine putting my sisters in danger like that. Maybe it was a twin thing? They were still young, too. We all think we're invincible in our teens. I turned to Landon. "What's the story with those two?"

"You know, they've worked with me for three years—since they were sixteen—and I still can't really say." He leaned back in his chair and stroked Mage's head. "They never talk about their home life. Last year, they moved into an apartment together, that's about all I know. Fearless, though. They'll try whatever trick I think up without a second thought."

Fearless or careless? "That trick with the spinning ropes is pretty impressive. So, are they gymnasts?"

"Nope. They are certified personal trainers and Tonya teaches a kickboxing class at the gym. But, like I said, they're up for anything."

"I can see where that would be necessary in a world of magic." I felt my mouth twitch. In a world where nothing... and no one is what it seems.

***

It was late when I got back. Karma was waiting for me at the door.

"You need to go out, boy?" His tail swished back and forth once. A *yes* in doggie language.

We walked across the road to the park. The air was still and thick and I had to keep swatting at the mosquitoes. I let Karma off the lead since the park was empty. "Hurry up, boy, before we get eaten alive out here."

He started sniffing the ground and then suddenly lifted his head, ears up and nose in the air. I thought it might be a squirrel when he trotted over to the big banyan tree. But as I moved to follow him, the shadow sitting on the ground was way bigger than a squirrel. Karma stopped for a second, then continued toward the shadow, ears down, tail wagging.

"Hello?" I called out.

"Hi, nice cookie lady!"

"Oh, hi, G." I stared down at him. He was rubbing Karma's chest. "What are you doing out here? You all right? You hungry?"

He gave Karma one last pat and then stood up. The familiar shoebox was tucked under his arm. "Had a muffin. And soup." He mumbled something else I couldn't understand as he reached into the box and pulled out a thick black sketch book. "Here." He lowered his head. "Mad Dog was your friend. Minnie says you should have what I found in the tent." He lifted his head. "It's all right if I keep the socks Minnie said."

I reached out and took the book. "Of course, G. You can keep the socks. Thank you for bringing this to me." I felt hope soar. This belonged to Mad Dog? There could be something important in here. I clutched it to my chest. "Hey, G?" He turned back to me. "You know I'm your friend, too, right?"

"Yep." He grinned, then ambled back through the park.

"Let's go see what Mad Dog can tell us, Karma."

***

Throwing my keys on the marble counter, I flipped opened the sketch book. A folded paper fluttered to the ground. Absentmindedly, I reached down and picked it up while still staring at the first page. It was a pencil drawing. A silhouette of a woman's face; long hair cascading over her bare shoulder, her lip turned up in a soft smile. Wow. Did Mad Dog sketch this? I flipped through the pages.

The first half was full of sketches of the same woman and also a little girl with large, dark eyes and wisps of dark hair around her ears. Some pages were just their eyes. One was of the woman's hand with a wedding band. One in particular struck me in the heart: the woman cradling the child, her eyes closed. Could this be his wife and daughter? I was awe struck and now more determined than ever to find Mariah. If only he had written the woman's name somewhere in the book. It would have made it easier to find them. I flipped through it again to make sure I hadn't missed anything. The last few pages made me sad. There were dark drawings of monsters with guns. Taped to the back cover was an envelope with "Mariah" written on it. I opened it to find a hundred dollars in twenties. I shoved the money back in the envelope and then unfolded the paper that had dropped out.

At the top in big black letters were the words: Release of Liability

The name, Frat Boys Inc., caught my eye. The corporation that owned the townhouse? I skimmed over it. It basically released the corporation from any claims, losses or damages due to injuries, permanent disabilities or...death. Participant acknowledges he/she is over the age of eighteen and understands the risks involved. I glanced down at the bottom signature line. It was blank.

Is this why Mad Dog said the injuries were his fault? Had he been involved in something he knew was dangerous? Something he was being paid for? I folded the paper back up. Tomorrow I would take it to Will and see what he thought.

TWENTY-SEVEN

"How do you look so cheerful and awake this morning?" I shook my head as Sylvia bounced through the boutique door, heels clicking gaily, her smile blinding me.

"It's a beautiful day, no?" She scratched Karma's head and began humming some tune as she tossed her keys and bag under the counter. I had a feeling someone hadn't slept alone last night. My cheeks grew warm with the thought.

"It's going to be a busy day, that's for sure. Landry Morrison is due any minute with her trio of terriers." I walked over to make a cup of green tea. I needed comfort.

"They are good babies. Oooo, and she brought cinnamon rolls last time."

How did Sylvia keep her figure with such a sweet tooth? As I moved back to the counter, the bells jangled. I was expecting Landry, but it was Will who strolled in.

"Oh, good morning." Wow. He was positively beaming. What was it with everyone this morning?

"These are for you." A bouquet of daisies appeared from behind his back. "Hi, Sylvia."

She waved and headed to the back, still humming.

"Awe, thanks." I pressed my nose into them. Sweet. "What's the occasion?"

"I have some good news."

"Good news? Great, I could use some of that. Want some tea?"

"No thanks." He followed me back to the counter.

"So, what's up?" I rested the daisies beside the computer. I'd take them upstairs and put them in a vase when I could.

"Mr. Fowler's murderer turned himself in last night. We got a full confession."

"What?" I couldn't have been more shocked if Mad Dog himself had walked through the door. I was not expecting this turn of events. "Who? I mean, that's great I guess but..." I was fumbling for the words. It just didn't make sense.

"You look like you just saw a ghost. You should be happy."

"Well. Yes. I guess I'm just shocked." I leaned against the counter for support. "Why would someone do that though? Turn themselves in? And why now?"

"I've learned not to try to figure out why people do what they do, Darwin. I just stick to facts. Otherwise, it'll drive you crazy."

"So, who was it?"

"A man named Richard Stranton. He knew Mr. Fowler from Pirate City. Seems there was an argument about money that resulted in a physical altercation. Says he didn't mean to kill him, he panicked when he realized Mr. Fowler wasn't breathing and pulled him into the lake to wash off any evidence and make it look like he drowned."

I crossed my arms. "A fight about money? And you believed him?"

"Well, the man confessed, Darwin. I thought you would be relieved."

Yeah, except there's no way that's what happened. "What about the bottle of expensive rum?"

"What about it? It obviously had nothing to do with Mr. Fowler after all. Someone just left it there."

Yeah, left it there to try and make it look like a drunk just fell in the lake and drowned. Only they didn't know Mad Dog. Besides, it was expensive rum. There's no way someone would just abandon it. I shook my head and glanced down at Karma stretched out on his pillow. His head was up and he was staring at us with those alert eyes.

"What about the fact there is no way Karma would stand by and let someone kill Mad Dog? He would have defended him. There would have been injuries on the man, on Karma or both."

Will eyed Karma and then looked back at me, smiling. "He doesn't have any teeth." I raised an eyebrow. He moved closer and rested a warm hand on each of my shoulders. "All right, look, Darwin, I know this a big chunk of news. I have to go, but I want you to process it, think about it and you'll see everything has worked out. It's the closure you've been after. You can let go."

Let go? "Oh wait," I gently released myself from his grip and went to dig in the drawer beneath the counter. "Before you go, can you tell me what this is?" I unfolded the paper from Mad Dog's notebook and handed it to Will. He read it over and nodded.

"Sure. It's a release of liability."

"Why would someone sign one?"

"Most places make you sign one if you're playing a sport on their property, or doing something dangerous like bungee jumping. Where did you get this?"

"From one of the guys at Pirate City. He found Mad Dog's sketch book and this was inside."

He handed the paper back. "Maybe this corporation was starting a sports company or something. I wouldn't worry about it. Besides," he put a finger under my chin and made me look up at him. "The person responsible for his death is in custody. You can stop playing detective now." He leaned down and kissed me. "I think we should celebrate tonight. Dinner?"

The door jangled again and Landry came in with three pink leashes in one hand and a bakery box in the other.

"Hello!"

Great, another cheerful soul. I was grateful for the interruption, though.

"Hi, Landry. Go on back. Sylvia's expecting you." I turned back to Will and gave him my best attempt at a smile. "I'll call you later."

"Promise?"

"Yes."

His phone vibrated, he kissed my cheek before answering it and heading out the door. My thoughts were whirling like a hurricane. Who was this person who confessed? Why would someone confess to a murder they didn't commit? How was I supposed to sit across from Will at dinner knowing what I knew about that night—that Mad Dog had been killed in the townhouse, not at the lake—and keep silent? I had to talk to this Richard Stranton person. Had I seen him at Pirate City before? It seemed they all go by nicknames so I had no idea who he was.

In between helping customers, I hatched a plan to visit Richard at the jail and confront him. I also began to work my way through the list of Fowlers in the Tampa area. I made it to listing number eight with no luck before Frankie came through the door with Itty and Bitty.

"Hey, Frankie." I felt disorientated. "I don't have you in the appointment book today?"

"No, no," she waved. "I just came by for some of those doggie truffles and to say hi. How's everything going?" She led the two pups over to the counter.

"Well, Will just stopped by with a shocking bit of news."

"Really? What's that?"

"Seems a man by the name of Richard Stranton turned himself in last night and confessed to killing Mad Dog."

"Well, I'll be a son of a sailor! That's great news!" Her hand was on her hip. "Right?"

"Sure." I tried to muster up her level of enthusiasm. "Will said the guy knew Mad Dog from Pirate City. You know anyone there by that name?"

She thought for a minute then shook her head. "No, sorry. But, I don't know if I actually know anybody's real name anyway."

"Yeah, that's why I'm going to go visit him at the jail and find out who he is and why he confessed."

"You don't believe he did it?"

"No."

TWENTY-EIGHT

It took twenty minutes to get to the Pinellas County Jail in a taxi that smelled like mold and feet. I had to make an appointment and, apparently, would only be allowed to speak with Mr. Stranton via video phone but that was probably for the best anyway. This way I wouldn't be arrested for strangling the man for lying.

After showing my ID, I was led to a row of visiting booths. I took a seat in a black plastic chair in front of a flat screen. There was a phone attached to the right side of the screen and it was bordered by a short privacy wall. My hands were damp and I rubbed them roughly on my shorts. I tried not to glance around at the other people visiting, but there really wasn't anywhere else to look. It seemed like forever before the screen flickered on and I was staring into the face of Richard Stranton. He had that same beaten down expression as when I had seen him last--sad eyes, droopy head.

I picked up the phone. "Hops?"

"Hey, I know you... Snow White, right? Why'd you come?"

"I need to ask you something." He just kept staring at me, so I laid it out. "I don't believe you're the one who killed Mad Dog. Why would you confess to it?"

"'Cause I did it. I killed him."

That sounded more like a rehearsed answer than a confession. "Then tell me this," I tried to keep my voice down, which was getting harder as my grip on my emotions slipped. "Tell me where his dog, Karma, was while this supposed confrontation happened?"

He shrugged. "How am I supposed to know where his dog was?"

"Because that dog would never leave Mad Dog's side. He would have been right there, in your face, if you hurt Mad Dog. Besides," my eyes narrowed. "You're a big guy but Mad Dog was a trained soldier. You wouldn't have got the best of him unless he was drunk or drugged, which the autopsy proved he wasn't."

Richard frowned and looked at me harder. "Why do you care so much?"

"Because I want the person responsible for his death behind bars. And you're not him."

We stared at each other for a long minute. Then his shoulders drooped and he looked away.

I didn't want him to end our conversation, so I tried a softer approach. "So, Mac was helping you with a resume the first time I saw you. Anything come of that?"

He made a noise like air seeping out of a tire. "There ain't no jobs for people like me. Hell, there ain't barely jobs for people who had college."

"Sure, it's tough out there but..." I sat up and stared at him. "Wait. Did someone give you money to take the blame?"

He glanced up at me. "I reckon our visit's over."

"Wait! Please!" I scooted closer to the screen. "You don't have to do this. I can pay you to tell the truth."

He hesitated, glanced from side to side, then offered me a sad smile. "Not enough. Miss, I get three meals a day in here and a roof over my head. No one needs to pay me no more. My worries are over. I'm retired."

I didn't even know what to say. I was still trying to wrap my mind around the idea of someone being so desperate for food and shelter they would confess to murder, when he hung up and disappeared. I hung up the phone on my end. Now what?

***

That evening I agreed to meet Will for dinner. I had been putting him off since Monday when he told me about Hop's confession. I knew I'd have to face him sooner or later. Time to put on my big girl pants, as Grandma Winters used to say.

Thick, gray clouds rolled across the sky, and it was pitch black to the east. A storm was coming. I decided to leave Karma home so we could eat indoors. Besides, wet dog was not my favorite fragrance.

Will was waiting for me outside Parkshore Grill. When I walked up, he enfolded me in a gentle hug, kissed the top of my head and then lifted my chin to kiss my mouth. I closed my eyes and let myself enjoy being in his arms. It was just a moment, though, before the guilt crept in and pushed me away from him like two positive sides of a magnet. I didn't deserve this. All the things I was keeping from him were between us and I couldn't let myself forget that. I couldn't be a hypocrite.

"Ready?" I asked, almost tearing up at the trust in those blue eyes and then at the confusion my sudden coolness caused.

"Sure." One word, whispered. He led me inside and we were seated at the same booth as when he first told me about the autopsy and about Mad Dog having a daughter. I was beginning to think of this as "our booth" and mentally smacked myself.

Will took a sip of water. "So, any luck finding information on Mr. Fowler's daughter?"

I glanced up. I swear the man could read my mind.

"No, not yet. I'm working my way through the phone book, calling all the Fowlers in the Tampa area. I spotted a Mariah Fowler there in a 4H article. I'm hoping it's her. Mad Dog sketched her, in the notebook. He must have really loved her and his wife. I can't imagine why he wouldn't be with them."

"There are all kinds of roadblocks life throws in people's way. Sometimes love's not enough."

"Feeling cynical tonight?"

"No. Just realistic."

Luckily, the waiter returned, because when I glanced at Will he looked painfully serious. I ordered the lobster pasta and Will ordered the shrimp capellini. The waiter left and Will slid his hand over mine.

"So, now that you're not going to be spending so much time searching for Mr. Fowler's murderer, maybe we can spend more time together."

I didn't like the way he was searching my face. Was he trying to figure out if I still believed they had the wrong guy? My body tensed. I was hoping to avoid this conversation, but who was I kidding? It was unavoidable.

"Will," I slipped my other hand on top of his. "Please don't get mad." I felt him pull back a little but I had to be honest with him, at least about this. "I went to visit Richard Stranton in jail."

He pulled his hands away and his face hardened. "Why would you do that?"

I held eye contact even though his darkening expression was killing me. "You know why."

He nodded and moved his gaze to stare outside. Raindrops were just starting to splatter on the sidewalk. The evening sky glowed sepia behind the dark clouds. "Because you don't believe he killed your friend."

I stayed silent, hoping he would think about this and realize it wasn't something that should come between us. But, his next words showed me why it would.

"You do realize that you are insulting my ability to do my job?"

"No!" I felt the heat crawl up my neck. "No, it's just that I know things..." *things you don't know.* "Like, I know Karma and he wouldn't have left Mad Dog's side. And when I talked to Hops... Richard Stranton, he said he confessed just to have a roof over his head and three meals a day. He wouldn't say that to you." *And I know that Mad Dog was killed at the townhouse, not the lake.* "It has nothing to do with your ability as a detective."

"Darwin, we didn't just accept his confession without question. There was a detail about the weapon used that we never released to the public. Richard Stranton brought the weapon with him, homemade brass knuckles with four triangles at point of impact. It matched the pattern of damage on Mr. Fowler's jaw and side exactly."

Well, that shut me up. For at least five minutes.

The waiter brought a bread basket and our salads. We picked at them in silence. I started thinking maybe Hops did kill him. But why would he lie about where it happened? I mean, if he was going to confess, why not confess the whole truth? I really needed Will's help to find out more about what kind of activities were going on in that townhouse. Maybe I could tell Will the truth about my vision. I snuck a glance at him. He looked so hurt. Was there a way to see how he felt about the subject first, without actually laying my soul bare and losing him forever?

"Hey, Will?"

"Yeah?"

"What about bringing in a psychic on the case? Does your department ever do that?"

Will's brows furrowed. "A psychic?"

I already didn't like his reaction, but I needed to know the depth of his disbelief or distain. "Yeah, you know, maybe they can give you some clues about what really happened that night. Wouldn't it be worth a shot?"

"First of all, our department does not use psychics or gypsies or fortunetellers, whatever you want to call those charlatans. And secondly, the case is closed. Did you even hear what I said about the homemade weapon?"

"Yes." Closed. Yep. The case and his mind. Well, that was that. I was on my own.

The rain dumped out of the night sky, pounding the sidewalk while we ate in silence, or pretended to eat. Even though the mouthfuls of warm, soft pasta were heaven, I was pretty sure we were both just trying to get the food past the lumps in our throats.

Will paid the check under my protest and held out his hand to help me out of the booth. Slipping my hand in his was pure torture. I felt the sweet, warm energy tingling up my arm into my chest.

We stood side by side at the front door. "Damn, I forgot an umbrella."

"I've got one, if you don't mind sharing." I dug in my straw bag and pulled out an umbrella. The second day I lived in St. Pete I purchased a pair of dark sunglasses and an umbrella. These are the two extremes we live in: blinding sun or soaking rain.

He looked down at me and when our eyes met, his mouth softened. "Look, Darwin, I'm sorry. I shouldn't have gotten so defensive. I don't want our night to end like this or my job coming between us. Forgive me?"

"Of course," I smiled, though he wasn't the one that needed forgiveness. My sin was much worse than a little anger. I was intentionally withholding information about myself that would change his mind about me. What did he call psychics? Charlatans? I definitely felt like a fraud. "Forgive me?"

"Of course. I'll walk you back home." He took the umbrella and opened the door. "Ready?"

I nodded and pressed against him as the umbrella popped open and we pushed out into the rain. Heavens, I loved these moments: Will's arm around me, my cheek pressed against his chest, immersed in the smell and sound of a summer storm. Oh, and no talking that would lead to hurt feelings. Too bad it was such a short walk.

"Is that Karma?" I asked, listening to a dog barking like mad. "Let me check the boutique." A gasp escaped me as we walked up. Will pulled me closer to him and we stared at the red letters spray painted on the windows.

"Stop medling bitch"

"Who would do that?"

"Someone who doesn't know how to spell." I touched the paint, it smeared. "Still wet. Creepy. Well, I better go get something to clean it off before it dries."

Will pulled out his phone and took a few pictures of the message. "I'll call a patrol car and stay with you until they get here."

"Do you think that's necessary? I mean, they didn't cause any permanent damage. It'll wash off."

"Yeah... this time. That's a threat though, Darwin. I take all threats seriously."

"All right, well, we can't stand out in the rain. Come on, we can wait for them upstairs."

As I led him through the gate, I mentally scanned the townhouse, trying to remember if I left anything out that might expose my secret. There were some candles on the coffee table, the water bowl on the kitchen counter. I had left my more incriminating items back home in Savannah. Still, my stomach tightened as we stood in the elevator side by side. Oh heavens. Maybe this wasn't such a good idea. Will smiled down at me. Too late now.

When I opened the door, Karma was right there, panting and pacing.

"It's okay, boy. The bad person is gone." I hugged his huge head and patted his rump to try and calm him down. Drool dripped onto my foot.

Ew. "Let's get a treat." As I stepped into the kitchen for Karma's peanut butter cookie, Will made his way into the living room and called the police on his cell. I heard him giving them the information and then he hung up and stood, looking out through the French doors. Karma swallowed his treat and lumbered over to stand beside him, ears alert. Two beautiful guardians.

"Great view. You have a lot of flowers out there."

"Yeah. Sort of a hobby." That wasn't really a lie was it? "Can I get you a drink while we wait for the police?"

"A glass of water would be fine, thanks." He turned around and, on his way over to the sofa, he picked up two candles off the floor and put them back on the coffee table.

"Thanks," I sighed, holding two glasses of water. "Karma must have knocked those off with his tail. This isn't the ideal decor for a hundred and fifty pound dog." We sunk down into the buttery leather couch.

"Do you plan on keeping him?"

I shrugged. "It never crossed my mind not to. I think he'd be kind of hard to adopt out with his special diet needs." I smiled as he licked the glass with a tongue the size of a man's shoe. "And I'd probably miss him."

"And he does windows. Bonus." Will laughed.

I moved my gaze from Karma to Will. His laugh was sunlight on my heart. And that smile... I sighed. He put his glass down and turned sideways on the couch to face me, then reached out a hand and stroked the back of my neck. The hair on my arms stood up. This was so dangerous. I was so much more susceptible to energy exchange during a storm. His energy flowed through me like a current of pure white hot fire. I had to keep my mind on why we were here.

"Will, do you think whoever painted that message was warning me to stop investigating Mad Dog's death?"

"All the more reason I'm glad it's over."

I lowered my eyes. Nope, not over for me. And maybe the real killer knows that. Was it just a coincidence I was threatened after visiting the man who was lying about killing Mad Dog? Or at least where he killed him?

"You're one of those girls who brought home stray animals, aren't you?"

"Guilty as charged." My words had a touch of breathlessness that I didn't recognize. Will apparently did. His blue eyes flashed and he slid next to me, his grip on the back of my neck tightening. My breath quickened more as his touch set every nerve ending in my body vibrating.

"That's what I love about you." I felt his words as hot breath on my lips and began to tremble. His lips brushed mine. He held my gaze as he pulled away and then moved in to press his mouth to mine. I moaned. I was a goner. His hands moved to hold my head as he kissed me with such a hunger, I was swept away from any awareness of time or space. The only thing that existed was this entangling of our mouths, this connection of our souls. When he pulled away— his lips glistening, his eyes half-closed—I took the opportunity to suck in a shuttering breath.

"You okay?" He stroked my arm and the sensation was almost painful. I suppressed another moan.

"Yeah, I," I tried to clear my head. "I forgot to wash off the paint." I had to get us off this couch, out of this secluded space where a wildfire could burn out of control. It would only make it harder when I had to let him go. But, I wanted to give him something, let him know how special he was to me. "I've never been kissed like that before."

He pushed a damp wave behind my ear and smiled. "Neither have I." Then he took my hand. "Come on, I'll help you clean the windows. The patrol car should be here any minute anyway."

"Let me take Karma down with us. He probably needs a bathroom break."

The cruiser pulled up while Karma was sniffing around the grass across the street. I watched Will greet them as they stepped out of the car. Oh great. It was Karma's two favorite policemen.

"Hurry up, Karma. I've gotta get you back inside."

Karma obliged and I held him close to me as we crossed the street. Halfway across he spotted the officers and I felt him grow a few inches taller as he held up his head, that rumbling starting in his chest.

"No. No growling." I stroked the ridge of fur standing up along his back. "It's okay, boy." I wrapped his lead tighter around my wrist and, as we approached, held up my free hand.

"Let me just put Karma upstairs. I'll be right back." He kept focused on the officers as I led him to the gate but didn't lunge toward them, thank heavens. I liked my arms *in* the sockets.

"Okay, sorry about that," I said, reappearing. "Karma doesn't seem to be too fond of y'all." I smiled.

Officer Hutchins scribbled in his notepad. He briefly looked up. "The feeling is mutual."

Will leaned down and whispered to me. "Cookie lady?"

Well, I see they had been busy. I whispered back. "Much more polite than my nickname for them, believe me."

We managed to make it through the next fifteen minutes without trading any more jabs, but I couldn't help but ask a final parting question.

"Officers? Did either of you have an altercation with Mad Dog before he died?"

They glanced at Will and then stared at me.

I wasn't about to be intimidated. "I'm just trying to figure out why Karma feels y'all are such a threat."

Officer Hutchins slapped his notebook shut and his mouth formed a smile that didn't move to his steely eyes. "Any more problems, give us a call."

"Might want to keep your girlfriend on a shorter leash. She's playin' in dangerous territory." Officer Cruz said to Will before sliding into the passenger side of the cruiser.

Girlfriend? I wanted to knock on his window and explain that I wasn't Will's girlfriend— although the thought did warm me inside—and also that I wasn't some animal to be put on a leash. The nerve.

"Don't worry about them." Will wrapped his arms around me. "They're harmless. All talk."

I pressed my forehead into his chest and sighed. Karma sure didn't think so. They had to have done something to Mad Dog in the past for him to react to them with such mistrust.

"Come on. I'll help you get those windows clean."

It took twenty minutes to wash and scrape the threatening message off. We were both drained from the emotionally volatile evening. We parted ways and I fell asleep on my bed in my clothes. I was definitely going to have to be more careful with my sleuthing.

TWENTY-NINE

The next evening, after we closed up the boutique, I took a walk to clear my head. My plan was to do some meditating down by the water but, as I strolled north down the sidewalk along Straub Park, I spotted Frankie talking to a man in front of the building housing the glass Chihuly Collection. They made a strange pair. Frankie's outfit consisted of red heels, zebra pants and a rhinestone baseball cap. The man was a hulking presence in a pair of dirty jeans with chains and a bandana. As I approached, Frankie handed him a shopping bag then he saluted, crossed the street and disappeared into the park.

I came up behind her. "Frankie?"

She whirled around and grabbed her chest. "Dear Lord, Darwin, you startled the hell out of me!"

"Sorry," I jerked my head in the direction of the park. "Who was that character?"

"Oh," she stared at me for a moment, thinking and then frowned. "That was Scary Harry." She watched my eyes widen and rested a hand on my shoulder. "The world is complicated, sweetie.

Come on up to my place and we'll have a glass of wine and some girl talk."

Her place turned out to be the entire top floor of one of the Vinoy Towers. We rode an elevator that opened right up into the five thousand square foot penthouse. Stepping inside nearly took my breath away. The gold and red walls, the huge chandeliers, the marble fireplace that sprouted from glossy cherry wood floors... the view.

"Holy Heavens," I managed through my gaping mouth.

"Here we go, home sweet home." Frankie smiled and bent over to pat Itty and Bitty as they ran up to us yipping. "Shush now, Mama's home. You gals hungry?" She moved toward a granite and stainless steel kitchen the size of a restaurant. "Let me feed the babies. Go on and have a look around."

I stood for a moment taking in the wide span of living space filled with décor fit for royalty and then my eyes moved straight out the massive windows to the blue sky and ocean.

"Oh, Frankie, it's simply amazing." I weaved my way through the leather strewn living room, drawn like a moth to light, to stare out through the glass. The entire side of the condo was glass. I had a tiny dizzy spell as I gazed out at the wrap around terrace. "Do you ever get tired of this view?"

"Haven't yet," she chuckled from the open kitchen. "We can sit out there and have our wine if you want."

"Sure."

"Go on out, I'll be there in a sec."

I opened the sliding door and stepped out into the warm evening breeze. It truly did feel like you were on top of the world here. As I settled into a wicker chair—grateful for the four foot curved glass barrier between me and a very long fall—I breathed in the salty air. It was such a blissful moment, I almost forgot why I had agreed to come. Almost.

"Couldn't you just die happy out here?" Frankie stepped out and handed me a full glass of chilled white wine. Itty and Bitty were at her heels. They circled her feet, then each other, finally settling down together on a large pink pillow in the corner.

I wasn't sure I liked her word choice, but she was right. Every bit of stress just melted away like a dream. This balcony was a bubble surrounded by sky and water that reality just couldn't touch.

We sat, sipping in silence for a few minutes before I finally had to break the spell.

"So, Scary Harry?"

She stretched out her legs and pushed the red heels off with her toes. "I know what it looked like. Like I was consorting with the enemy, right?"

"Yeah."

"See, the thing is, the man is mean as a snake. He's not gonna stop messin' with my family at Pirate City. And the police aren't doing anything about his harassment. So," she shrugged, "I'm paying him off."

"You're giving him money?"

"Well, no, not money per say—liquor. He likes expensive liquor, so I agreed to buy it for him once a week and he agreed to leave Pirate City alone. Tell you the truth, I hope he drinks himself to death. Waste of human flesh, that man."

Well, that was a relief. Pirate City was safe, at least from Harry, at least for now. Something nagged at my thoughts. I went back over Frankie's words. Oh, yeah... expensive liquor.

"How long have you been giving him this liquor?"

"Oh, we just struck the deal this week."

"Oh, okay." It was worth a shot.

"Why's that?"

"Well, when they found Mad Dog, there was a bottle of Bacardi 8 rum lying in the grass. I thought maybe we could connect it to Harry."

I could feel Frankie staring at me, I turned to her. "What?"

"Did you say Bacardi 8?"

"Yeah?"

"Huh. Well, I did have a bottle of that go missing, but it was weeks before Mad Dog got killed. Still, there's not many of those bottles floating around."

"Who do you think took it?"

"I chalked it up to Vick. I mean, I didn't really care, he knew he could take it if he wanted it. Just seems like a big coincidence." She got lost in thought.

"Frankie?"

"Hm?"

"Please don't get mad at my next question, okay?" I seemed to be saying that a lot lately. "I'm just trying to cover all the possibilities. But, do you think Vick could have had something to do with Mad Dog's death that night?"

"No. And don't get me wrong, I know he's not the most moral guy in the world, he's got his faults. But, he was here all night. He left in the early morning, to go back to his place, and called me when he passed Mirror Lake and saw all the police cars."

I nodded, remembering she had told me that before. "How are y'all doing? You and Vick?" I wanted to ask what in heaven's name she saw in him, but I remembered my manners.

"I don't know. He's been acting kinda weird lately. We got in a fight at the benefit and since then, he's been standoffish."

"Well, you're great fun to be around, Frankie. There's plenty of other fish in the sea."

"Thanks, but you know the hardest thing about having money is dating. You can't trust anybody. You always have it in the back of your mind that they're only in it for the money."

"And Vick is different?"

She nodded and took a sip of her wine. "I knew him before I had money. Plus, he's got his own money. Of course, that was a big part of our fight. I wish he'd give up his business. I don't like it one bit."

"His computer business?"

She glanced at me sideways. I recognized the action. She wanted to tell me more but didn't know if she could trust me. So, I prodded a bit. "You said he sells stuff online? Is it not legal? Is that why you don't like it?"

"Oh, it's legal." She shook her head and squinted out at the blue sky. "Damn well shouldn't be." She squirmed in her chair and then pushed herself up. "Hey, I'll just get us a snack. I've got some fresh sushi and watermelon in the fridge."

I started to protest, but she had already slipped inside. Itty and Bitty jumped up to follow her. I sighed. Probably wouldn't be able to get her back onto that topic again tonight. Now she had me really curious, though. What in the world could Vick be selling online that was legal but upset Frankie enough to fight with him about it?

"Here we are." She appeared back through the door with plates of fresh food, laying them out on the glass table between us. "Go lay down girls, this is for the big people."

"You shouldn't have gone to all this trouble."

"Are you kiddin'? This is no trouble. Glad to have the company."

I smiled at Frankie as I popped a juicy piece of watermelon in my mouth. She really did seem like a kind soul. Someone who just wanted to enjoy what life had so thoughtfully tossed into her lap and share some of that good fortune with others.

"Oh!" I swallowed. "I haven't told you the latest news. So, I went and visited the guy who confessed to killing Mad Dog in jail and it was Hops."

"Hops?" Frankie frowned. "I can't imagine him killin' anyone."

"I know. So, he basically told me he confessed so he'd have a roof over his head and three meals a day. Can you believe it?"

Frankie's eyes saddened. "Yeah, I can, sugar. He was gettin' pretty desperate. Couldn't find work. It gets tough out there. So, you're really convinced he didn't kill Mad Dog then?"

"Well, I was." It was my turn to frown. "Until Will told me that Hops turned in a weapon, homemade brass knuckles that matched the impact points on Mad Dog's head and side exactly. So, I guess he must have killed him. But not at the lake like he said. Why would he lie about that?"

"How do you know it wasn't at the lake?"

Oops. "Oh, um, just something he said. Made me think that." Squirm. "So, anyway, I just can't let it go yet. I have to know for sure that Mad Dog's real killer is the one paying for the crime. Hops as the killer just doesn't feel right."

Frankie wagged a finger at me. "You know, if you were a dog, you'd be a pit bull, Darwin. You just sink your teeth into something and don't let go. I'll remember that next time I have a problem that I'm not gettin' solved."

We laughed together and munched a few California rolls in silence. Then Frankie sighed, "Maybe you could find out where in Hades Maddy's gone to. Now her phone is cut off. I even went by her apartment and she's moved out."

I thought about the card with her name on it in Vick's truck and the vision I had of Vick with his hands around her neck. "Sounds like she has some personal problem she's running from. Sometimes you just have to go somewhere and start over."

"I know. But, I wish she would have at least kept in touch with me." She took a deep drink and drained her wine glass. "And while we're on sad topics. You remember Junior, the junkie who fell in the pool at the charity event?"

"Of course."

"He overdosed. Pops got him to the hospital but it was too late." She shook her head. "I really tried to help that kid. Sometimes it's too late before you start."

I guess I shouldn't have been shocked, but I was. I thought back to the time I first saw him at Pirate City, then at the Mirror Lake morning breakfast and then Will pulling him out of the pool. "So, he got out of the hospital and went right back to drugs?" Was this reality here? I wasn't used to all this death.

"Yep."

"He was so young." Where was his family? "Was there a funeral?"

"No. He had no next of kin written on the Pirate City wall. He'll be cremated and I've asked for the ashes so we can have a proper goodbye and give him to the Bay. He loved boats. Always talked about wantin' one someday."

"Will you let me know when you have it? I'd like to be there."

"Sure thing. If I can pick up his remains tomorrow, I'll rent us a boat Saturday morning."

"Okay." Night was falling with our mood. "Well, I should get home to let Karma out. Thanks for having me over, this place is amazing."

Frankie stood up and walked me to the door. So did Itty and Bitty. "Anytime, sugar. I'll let you know about Saturday." We hugged and I stepped back into the elevator.

The walk home seemed lonely and I almost called Will. What could we talk about though? All my energy right now belonged to finding out the truth about the night Mad Dog was killed, and he considered that topic closed.

Instead I went home and fell asleep with one arm draped across Karma, whispering to him that I was still keeping my promise. He stopped snoring and licked my arm. At least somebody thought I was doing the right thing.

THIRTY

True to her word, Frankie called Friday to say that she picked up Junior's ashes and had chartered a boat. I was to meet her and the others at the Municipal Marina at 9 a.m. Saturday morning. She said I could bring Karma along, so we headed to the marina to find the crew.

As we walked the docks, surrounded by a sea of sailboats, I spotted Frankie waving to me from the deck of a ginormous white boat. I waved back. A gentleman in a white uniform helped me and Karma aboard.

Frankie hugged me tight. She wore a black silk suit, flats and oversized dark sunglasses.

"Glad you could make it. The gang is inside." She turned to the man. "This is Captain Manning." We shook hands and he patted Karma. "Okay, Darwin is our last expected guest. We can shove off."

"Yes, ma'am."

I followed Frankie into a living room of sorts, all warm and decked out in cherry wood and crème leather furniture. A bundle of white roses lay on the glass coffee table. Despite the fact that they were sitting around on what was probably a million dollar yacht, the gang was in a solemn mood. Mac was there. On either side of him sat Minnie and Pops. The kid with the blonde dreadlocks sat beside Pops and there was a young Hispanic girl I didn't recognize. They looked uncomfortable, sitting around on the couch with their hands in their laps. The only one who seemed at home was Vick. He was leaning on the glossy wood bar two steps up, looking down at us. His usually pulled back hair hung free, a gold cross glittered in the V of his open shirt. I quickly decided to ignore him for as long as I could.

"Hi, y'all." I held up a hand and offered them a consoling smile. "So sorry about the loss of Junior. He was so young." Some of them nodded or smiled back. Karma sniffed around on the floor and then moseyed over to Pops, head down, tail slightly wagging.

"Hey, Snow White." Pops rubbed Karma's back. "And Karma. Good to see you, boy."

I noticed they had all done their best to dress nicely with combed back hair and scrubbed faces. I was kind of disappointed not to see G among them. He always made me smile and I wanted to thank him for giving me Mad Dog's sketch book and let him know how important it had turned out to be.

I took a seat on the edge of the curved couch. Karma came over and plopped down at my feet. "Where's G?" I asked Frankie.

"Oh, he's afraid of boats. Couldn't get him to come."

Minnie reached in her pocket and pulled out a blue bandana. "G asked me to throw this in the water for Junior. It was his favorite."

The pirate boy made a hissing sound then said, "Waste of a perfectly good bandana."

"You hush up, Rufus." Mac growled. "Have some respect for a brother's wishes."

"Can I get anyone coffee, juice or water?" Frankie moved toward the steps.

Most of them asked for coffee. The girl I didn't know asked for orange juice. I opted for water. Vick followed Frankie passed a formal dining area and into the dark granite kitchen. I felt the boat rumble around us as it began to pull away from the dock. It was a strange sensation.

I noticed a beat up guitar leaning against Rufus' leg. "You play guitar, Rufus?"

"Yeah."

"He wrote a song to sing for Junior," Minnie said, while Rufus glanced at me uncomfortably.

"That true?" I asked.

"Yeah. No big deal."

"Well, I think that's nice." I offered my hand to the girl next to me. "Hi, I'm Darwin Winters."

"Oh, Aleece." Her hand was soft and damp. "Nice to meet you."

I didn't remember seeing her at Pirate City. "You were a friend of Junior's?"

"Yeah, we hung out. He was nice to me."

I automatically checked her arms to look for signs of drug use. There were none and then I felt bad. "Well, I'm sorry you lost your friend. I know how it feels. I lost a friend from Pirate City,

too. He was murdered. This was his dog, Karma."
I patted Karma's head and, panting, he rolled his
eyes in our direction. "I promised him I'd find out
who took Mad Dog away from us."

"You promised the dog?" she asked.

I nodded. Frankie and Vick came back down
with the drinks.

Aleece frowned at me. "Junior told me that
Hops guy confessed to killing Mad Dog during a
fight. That he's in jail for it."

"Yeah, I know." I accepted the water bottle
from Frankie. I could feel the yacht picking up
speed, pushing forward through the water. "I'm
not convinced that's what really happened
though."

"Oh." She took a glass of orange juice from
Vick's hand. "Thanks. Wow, really?"

I happened to glance over at Mac and his eyes
were locked on me. He shook his head slightly
and sipped his coffee, still staring at me over the
cup. Was that a warning?

Everyone seemed to get quiet. Frankie finally
broke the silence.

"Now's a good time to be thinking if you want
to say a few words when... you know, we let
Junior go. I know Rufus's got a song and Aleece
has a poem she wants to read." She smiled kindly
at Aleece. "The captain will stop in about fifteen
minutes and we'll go on up. Apparently, the law
says we have to stay within three miles of shore."

It only took about ten minutes for the yacht
to cut through the open sea to a place where it
was legal to release human remains. We each

took a flower off the table and filed past the kitchen and up the couple of plush stairs to the birthing area on top. The sea sparkled around us and the salty breeze tugged at our clothes. I tried my best to block the waves of sadness coming at me from all directions but it was hard. The surrounding water was like an amplifier for their emotional energy.

Frankie led the group, carrying the box containing Junior's remains. We all gathered around solemnly in front of her as she stopped at the railing and turned to face us. I noticed Vick had wandered over a few feet away from her and stayed facing the ocean. I guess he wasn't one for ceremony.

"Thanks, everyone, for coming to say goodbye to Junior. The kid had a tough life. I hate that it had to end like this and I know you do, too. I'm sure he's lookin' down on us now, smiling and happy to know that he had people who genuinely cared about him. Aleece, why don't you start us off with the poem you wrote for him?"

Aleece nodded and took a few unsteady steps to stand beside Frankie. She unfolded a piece of paper she had been clutching and began to read:

> "To my friend, Junior,
> We never know when we'll find
> A person who is thoughtful and kind,
> And even though you had no home
> You made me feel like I wasn't alone,
> You listened to me and made me smile

I didn't know that all the while
Your time on earth was almost done
I'll miss you more than anyone."

She folded the paper back up, wiped at her eyes and transferred a kiss from her hand to Junior's makeshift urn.

"Thank you, Aleece. That was beautiful." Frankie squeezed her shoulder before she came back to the group. "I think this just goes to show us, no matter how down we are in life, we can still have meaningful friendships. Now Junior's memory will live on with Aleece and that didn't cost any money at all." She took a deep breath and invited Mac up. As he told a few anecdotal stories about his time with Junior at Pirate City, I turned my attention to Vick. He had moved further away from us and had his hands shoved in his pockets, still staring out at the ocean. I would have given anything to know what was going through his mind at that time. Something important by the look of his concentration. Was he thinking about Maddy? I suddenly got a not-so-bright idea. I decided to poke the rattle snake.

After Minnie and Pops said a few words and Rufus sang his song, Frankie said, "It's time."

We all moved to the railing on either side of Frankie as she opened the box, said a little blessing and dumped Junior's remains over the side. As the breeze carried the ashes out to mingle with the choppy water, we tossed the white roses into the sea after them. Minnie also tossed the bandana.

We stood there in silence, watching the roses bob around on the surface. It was very peaceful. I suddenly remembered Mad Dog's ashes were still in storage. Should I have a ceremony for him, too? No, he had a family. They deserved to be there, to have closure. I was more determined than ever to find them.

One by one, the gang peeled themselves away from the railing and went back below deck. I held back, waiting.

"That was lovely," I told Frankie as she wiped at her eyes under her dark glasses.

"Thanks for being here, Darwin." She squeezed my hand. "All we can hope for is that someone will care when we're gone, I suppose."

"While we're alive is nice, too." I watched her descend the steps and saw Vick making his way over. "Come on, Karma." I tilted my head to watch him as he pushed himself off the deck. He was moving slow. I should have given him some flower essence for sea sickness. I waited by the stairs. Karma lumbered down first. I took my time. When I felt Vick coming up behind me, I turned to face him.

"I know about Maddy." I said it simply and waited.

He had a good poker face. Stillness, except for a widening of the eyes. Then they narrowed and flashed with anger.

"I don't know what you're talking about." He pushed past me, almost knocking me over.

"Temper temper," I whispered. After regaining my balance, I joined the others on the couch. Vick stood in the kitchen, his back to us.

Now I really would give anything to know what was going through that sleazy mind. Did he think I was going to tell Frankie? Maybe he would confess to her first. What would he confess to? An affair? Arguing and almost strangling Maddy?

Karma sat up and rested his head on my lap. He was panting hard and foaming drool oozed onto my bare leg. "Um, Frankie... I don't think Karma's feeling well. Can we get him some water?"

"Sure thing, sugar." She dug through the cupboards. I heard her turn on the faucet but it was too late. At least Karma was courteous enough to lift his head off my lap before he yakked all over the million dollar yacht.

THIRTY-ONE

Sylvia breezed into the boutique Monday morning with a glimmer of hope for me.

"This one," she tapped a burgundy nail on a circled phone number, "I think knows something." Her eyes sparkled as she flicked her dark hair off a shoulder. "I say, 'May I speak to Mariah Fowler.' And the woman, she pauses for a long time. I say, 'Hello?' She says, 'Who's asking?'"

My breath quickened. "And what did you say?"

"I say, 'A friend of her fathers.' Then she disconnect!"

"Aha!" The world seemed brighter suddenly. I hugged Sylvia. "Oh, you're the best. She must know Mad Dog."

"Maybe yes, maybe no." Sylvia rested a hand on my shoulder. "But, you must promise me the only thing you are doing now is this. Find his daughter. No more putting yourself in danger, my *bom amiga*."

I knew she was worried. I hadn't ever seen her as rattled as she was when I told her about the message spray painted on the boutique window. Then mad as a hornet. Fear for her definitely translated into anger. I wasn't afraid yet. Sylvia says I'm naïve. Maybe. But, naïve or not, I believed in helping those who couldn't help themselves. And the dead fell into that category.

I couldn't promise her that. I distracted her with a broad smile instead. "I will try to stay out of trouble."

She shook her head and leveled a hard stare at me. "You promise?"

Luckily, our first customer of the day came through the door and saved me. As Sylvia chatted with her, I scooped up the paper with the circled number and dug out my cell phone. Each ring made my heart pump faster. No one picked up. After the beep, I took a deep breath and tried to sound calm and friendly.

"Hi, my name is Darwin Winters. I own Darwin's Pet Boutique in St. Pete and am looking for a little girl named Mariah Fowler. She would be about nine years old. I was really hoping not to leave this kind of message on an answering machine, but I'm afraid you won't call me back if I don't. I'm a friend of her father's, Mad… Matthew Fowler. I'm sorry to say that he's deceased. I have something from him I'd like his daughter to have. It's a sketch book full of drawings. If I do have the right number, please call me back." I left my number. When I ended the call, I noticed I had a message.

It was from Will. I listened to it twice, just to hear his voice.

"Hi, Darwin. It's me. Listen, I talked to Officer Hutchins and found out that he and his partner did arrest Mr. Fowler at one time for loitering. He said Karma was there when they put him in the back of the police car, barking at them, but he ran off. I knew you'd still be worried about Karma's reaction to them so, well, just thought it would give you an explanation. Ease your mind a bit." There was a pause. "I'm free on Thursday evening if you'd like to have dinner. Give me a call. I'd like to see you."

I hung up feeling sad. He really knew me. I mean, as much as I'd let him know me. He knew that I needed closure, I needed explanations. And he went out of his way to give that to me. Wow. I think that was about the kindest thing anyone's ever done for me. Any male for sure.

I called him back and left a message that I would have dinner with him. Karma huffed on his pillow. "You can go too, boy. We'll eat outside."

"Glad I'm not the only one who talks to my dogs." Betsy Mills, the real estate mogul with the three standard poodles—one in each color—stood grinning at me with the reddest lipstick I have ever seen on a woman. I couldn't stop staring at her mouth.

"Oh, Hi, Miss Mills. What can I do for you today?" I tried to hold my gaze to eye level but it kept slipping back down to her clown mouth. *Stop it Darwin, that's rude.*

"Well, my boys just tremble every time a storm rolls through here, and Frankie tells me you have something to help them with their nerves."

"Sure, it's flower essence. I can get that for you. Browse around a bit. I'll be right back."

I grabbed some aspen and impatient bottles and brought them back up to her. As I wrapped her flower essence and rang up the pile of other things she had found to pamper her pooches, I got curious. "Miss Mills, there's a townhouse on Fifth Avenue that's owned by a corporation and I'm trying to get in touch with the owner. You being a real estate agent and all, do you think you could help me with that?"

"If it's been sold in the last ten years, it was probably my sale. What's the address?"

Address. Shoot. "Oh, I don't know. I'll have to get back to you with it."

"Sure, be glad to help if I can. If you're in the market for a place, I've got some amazing properties for sale right now. Great deals, too." She dug a business card out of her wallet and handed it to me. I did a double take because the woman in the photo appeared about twenty years younger.

I bit my tongue. "Thank you, Miss Mills. Appreciate it." I slipped the card into my pocket and gave her instructions on how to use the flower essence.

After she left, I grabbed a cup of tea and stared out at Beach Drive, thinking. It would be nice if Miss Mills could find out for me but I couldn't wait for her. I had to find out who owned the townhouse where Mad Dog died. It was up to me now.

THIRTY-TWO

Wednesday evening, we closed up the boutique at six and I decided to take Karma to visit the gang at Pirate City. Okay, so I had an ulterior motive. I had been thinking: somebody there had to know who was beating up Mad Dog and Junior before they died. And then I had a horrible thought. What if Mad Dog's murderer also killed Junior and made it look like a drug overdose? A cover-up just like they tried to do with Mad Dog? Mac definitely knew something he wasn't telling me. I had to get him to talk to me.

So, I stuffed my back pack with half a boiled, sliced roast—which Karma pouted about—a bag of carrots and celery, a big jar of almond butter and, of course, a few baggies of oatmeal raisin cookies and we set off; me on my bike, Karma trucking along beside me.

When we reached the dead end road, Karma started acting a bit nervous. He had his ears up and stood in his alert posture, scanning the area around us. I glanced around too. It was a beautiful late afternoon. No sign of wild boar or any other trouble.

I shrugged. "Come on, boy." I led him down the path and unhooked his lead once we got into the camp.

"Yo, Snow White!" Pops waved to me from his position at the plywood table where about a dozen of the fellows were playing cards. I walked over and let Karma sniff around. "You want us to deal you in?"

"Maybe next time. Just brought some leftovers for y'all, can't stay long." I unpacked my back pack and put the food in the middle of the table, keeping the smallest bag of cookies aside for G. So, what's new? G here?"

"G's in his tent. Hey, Neddy Dean here got himself a job working on bikes."

I smiled at the man he nudged beside him. "Well look at you. Congratulations."

His brown eyes set deep in pocked brown skin looked tired but happy. "Thanks. Not enough pay to get me out of this place yet but it's somethin'."

"You're buying the beer this week," Rufus said, digging into the roast. Some of the others followed.

I stared at Rufus, my heart dropping like a rock. The whole left side of his face was purple and swollen. Now *he* was involved in whatever was going on? I wanted to both hug him and shake him. But I knew if I couldn't get Mad Dog to tell me what was going on, Rufus would definitely be a dead end. Bad pun. I had to turn away. "All right, I'm going to go visit with G now."

Karma stuck close by me as I walked over to the red and white tent that used to be Mad Dog's.

"G? You in there?" Hmm. No place to knock. Not necessary, though, as it turned out. G came busting out through the opening like a kid on Christmas morning. I couldn't help but smile.

"Cookie Lady!" His toothless grin and shiny eyes reminded me of Karma's.

"Hi, G." I held out the bag of oatmeal cookies. "I wanted to thank you for giving me Mad Dog's sketch book. It was very helpful."

He took the bag, opened it and stuck his nose inside. "Mmmmm. Smells good." Then he looked up at me, wrinkles appearing on his leathery forehead. "You want the socks?"

"No, G," I assured him. "The socks are yours."

"Okay." He nodded, smiled and disappeared back into his tent with the cookies. I heard him start singing as I walked away. Some heavy emotion clutched at me but I pushed it aside. It was time to talk to Mac.

I found him sitting under the blue tarp at his desk, his grey hair pulled back in a ponytail, his arms crossed. He looked up when I entered and gave me a half-hearted nod.

"Hey, Mac." I sat in the plastic chair across from him and Karma sat beside me, pressing up against my leg. I rested a hand on his back. "How's things?"

"Quieter without Junior." He shook his head. "You always hope the young ones will get out some day. Just not like this."

"It's not too late to help Rufus. Tell me what's going on here. Let me help."

He turned away. We sat in silence for a moment and I could hear the katydids and frogs singing their little hearts out. Desperation made me impatient.

"Mac? Please. I saw Rufus's face. Obviously it wasn't Hops beating up Mad Dog because it's still going on. I know you don't want Rufus to end up like him."

Reluctantly, he met my gaze. "Darwin," he shook his head, "I can't. I don't want you endin' up dead, neither, and you are already in danger."

It was the first time he had used my real name and that startled me more than his declaration that I was in danger. Whatever layer of protection the nicknames gave them from getting close to each other had now vanished between us. He was speaking directly to me with no wall. I instinctively knew this was as serious as he could get. Still, I shook it off.

"I can take care of myself, Mac. Besides…" I smacked at a mosquito on my leg and then threw up my hands. "How do you know that Junior wasn't killed? Someone could have forced him to overdose or given him bad drugs. This has got to end."

He sighed. "These people make their own choices and live with their own consequences. Hell, some of 'em come here because, for one reason or another, they don't want society telling them how to live. They live and die by their own rules. That's the code here. We don't dictate each other's lives."

"But you care… you help each other. Whether you like it or not, this is a faction of society. You do have a responsibility to your fellow man. And I don't buy for one second that you don't care, that you're willing to sit back and do nothing when you know a friend is in danger."

He set his jaw. "You're wrong. I don't care." He lit a citronella candle, picked up a pen and refused to look at me. "Best be on your way, Snow White."

I stood up, wiping the salty sweat and a stray tear off my cheek and left silently with Karma still stuck to me like glue. The sun had already dropped like a rock. I waved goodbye to the guys at the table and then moved down the path more by memory than sight. The moon was no help tonight. The bugs and frogs had gotten louder, bolder in the darkness. The crackling of branches, Karma's panting, everything seemed louder.

We emerged from the end of the path and I snapped Karma's lead back on him. Just then, his breath halted and he stared toward the dead end circle. The low growl began in the barrel of his chest. He woofed almost silently. I lifted my head and peered down toward the dead end circle. I could make out the hulking shape of a car parked there. Oh great. Officer Hutchins and his partner must be on stake out.

I led my bike and Karma out into the road and waved at the officers in case they could see us.

"It's okay, Karma." I tried to turn him away but he stood his ground. Heavens, he was strong. I was afraid if I got on my bike, I wouldn't be able to pull him along so I just inched it forward, tugging on Karma's lead. "Let's go, boy."

Just then the car started, its lights flicked on.

Oh no, please don't bother us tonight. There's no way I could hold Karma back as worked up as he was.

The engine began to rev. *Vroooom! Vroooom!*

I only had a second to ponder this before the tires screamed and smoke blossomed as the car came barreling at us, somebody mashing the gas pedal for all they were worth.

Karma ripped the lead out of my hand and took off toward the car. Without thinking, I took off right after him. "Karma! Stop!"

The impact truly was painless and silent—except for the horrifying sound of Karma's scream.

THIRTY-THREE

A cold, heavy blackness clung to me. I focused on the beeping sound, pulling my consciousness toward it. Why can't I open my eyes? Why is it so cold? Voices! Hello? I can hear you talking.

Am I dreaming? No one was answering me and I couldn't move my arms. Something stiff gripped my neck. Fingers pressed into my scalp. Ouch. Stop please! That hurts. The fingers gratefully complied.

A siren shrieked and I realized I was floating, moving fast. A bump. Two bumps.

The fingers returned, pressing along my right rib cage then deep into my abdomen. There were voices but they were just noise. I couldn't make sense of the words. Why was it so cold? I was powerless to stop the trembling in my own body.

I tried to reach back—back into the darkness to figure out where I was.

Oh yeah! I was talking to Mac at Pirate City. He wasn't going to help me. Wait. I left, I walked down the path, right?

I... OH. MY. GOD. The car lights! That terrible squealing then crunching sound and...

Karma!

Karma!

I was screaming, why couldn't they hear me? I can't move! Please, I have to help Karma. My arms weren't lifting. Help me! Stop talking about my heart rate! Oh no. Please…

***

A female voice drifted into my consciousness along with a low, consistent beeping. I breathed in the sweet scent of flowers. My finger moved and stroked soft material. I reached up and swatted at something in my nose. Too much effort. Darkness closed in.

***

"Darwin? Darwin? Can you hear me?"

My eyes fluttered open. Where am I? I attempted a smile as Sylvia's face came into focus above me. She looked so worried. Tiny creases marred her skin between perfectly plucked brows. *Don't worry, I'm fine.* It would take too much effort to say this out loud. I felt her rest a cool hand on my cheek.

"It's going to be okay, you *assustado nós tudo.*" Her lips brushed my forehead. My eyelids were lead and I couldn't hold them open. "You rest." Her words carried me back into the comforting darkness.

Drifting in and out of reality, it became hard to decide which was which. Vivid dreams of swimming deep in the ocean, breathing and talking beneath the water haunted me. So real, though.

In this underwater world, my father was there. I hadn't seen him since I was nine years old, but I recognized him all the same. He wore a black suit and glowed with a purple light. He clicked his tongue at me and told me I must be careful, that my mother would not be happy if I left this world so soon. A woman floated next to him. Well, not a woman really... more like half woman, half fish with wild long hair that pulsed with energy. Her hand rested on a large wolf with glowing green eyes.

It went on like this for I don't know how long. Each push into the real world brought something new: a dull pain to my side, a pulsing in my head, a sharp memory of Karma and no way to know what happened to him, sunlight slanting through plastic vertical blinds, a cry that no one could hear, an unfamiliar voice, Frankie's voice, the smell of antiseptic, the particular stillness of midnight. My eyes, so heavy. My body, so tired.

Finally, the moment came when I became aware of being awake and I could hold my eyes open, hold my mind steady to take in the room. I was in the hospital hooked up to an IV bag, my legs and arms heavy beneath a blue gown and crème blanket. My head was foggy and sore. The light coming through the blinds held the silver quality of morning. The air kicked on with a loud clunk. How long had I been in here? I turned my head slowly to peek at the door over the vases full of flowers. It clicked open.

"Well, look who's up this morning." A gray haired nurse busied herself around me, checking the bags and machines and my vitals. "I'm Margie. How are you feeling?"

I croaked out a reply but it came as a dry whisper. She poured water from the pitcher into a cup and pushed a button to raise my bed. "Just sip. It's been a few days since you've put anything in your stomach."

A few days? I took a small drink and cleared my throat. "How many days?"

"You came in on Wednesday evening. It's Saturday morning."

I lost two whole days? What about the boutique? What about Karma?

"My dog? Did he survive?"

Her grey eyes flicked toward me. "I'm sure a family member or friend will be around soon and you can ask them. You've had quite the parade of visitors."

My stomach cramped and I squeezed my eyes closed.

"How's your pain level? You've got a little button right here if you need to increase the morphine." She rested it by my hand. "You've got some serious bruising and abrasions to the whole right side of your body, but nothing broken. A mild concussion and some stitches at the scalp line. You can try some solid food when you feel ready. We'll do a sponge bath later and change your gown."

I nodded and felt myself fading back into the blackness. Karma's sweet face came into focus. I wrapped my arms around him. *I'm so sorry, boy.*

The next time I awoke, I heard humming. I rolled my head toward the window and forced my eyes open. Frankie sat in the chair, her head back, humming to herself.

"Hi," I managed.

She jumped out of the chair. "Darwin! Oh thank Jesus!" She pulled the chair up beside the bed and looked at me like she wanted to hug me but was afraid. "How are you feeling? You scared the devil out of us, sugar."

"I'll be fine. Frankie?" I didn't really want to hear it, didn't want it to be true, but I had to know. "Karma?"

She forced a smile but her eyes looked sad. "I've got the vet's number right here. Figured you'd want to talk to 'em as soon as you were awake."

"Is he... alive?"

"Yes." Her hesitation worried me, but at least he was alive. That was more than I could hope for.

"Would you mind dialing it for me?"

"Sure." She dug out her cell phone, dialed and placed the phone on the pillow next to my ear.

"Emergency Veterinary, Donna speaking."

"Hi, Donna. My name is Darwin Winters. I'm Karma's owner. We were hit by a car on Wednesday and I need to check on him."

"Certainly, Miss Winters. I'll get the vet for you."

After listening to elevator music for a few minutes, which almost put me back to sleep, a woman came on the line. "Hi, Miss Winters. I'm Dr. Messing. I understand you are Karma's owner?"

"Yes." I stared at Frankie for support.

"Okay, well, I'll give you the rundown of his injuries and what we've done so far. The most serious injuries were internal. He had a lacerated lung and a ruptured spleen which caused internal bleeding. We did emergency surgery to repair those and now just have to watch for signs of infection. We also had to repair a broken front leg with metal pins. He's got a pretty good size laceration to the bone in his chest that we've sutured and multiple other cuts that will heal on their own."

Nausea started to overwhelm me and I squeezed my eyes shut in an effort to control it. I couldn't imagine how scared and confused he must be, in pain for days without knowing if I was ever coming for him. "Will he be okay?"

"Well, he's still in critical condition and if he survives, he will have a recovery period, will need IV fluids administered at home. But a few positive things, he's not showing any signs of head trauma or spinal cord injury. And the fact that he doesn't have any teeth probably saved his tongue and gums, dogs usually seize when they get hit and bite into their mouths."

Thank heavens for small favors. "Okay. I'm still in the hospital, so I can't pick him up."

"It's okay. He's not ready to go home yet."

"You have my permission to do whatever it takes to help him. I'm not worried about the cost. Can I give you a number to keep me updated?"

"Sure, and call anytime to check on him."

"Thank you, Dr. Messing." I gave her my cell number and after I hung up, I realized I didn't have any of my belongings. "He's in pretty bad shape but I feel like they're doing what they can for him. How did he get to the vet? And how did I get here?"

"Oh, Mac and the gang heard the accident, heard the tires squeal and heard Karma yelp. The car was already around the corner when they found you, so they didn't get a look at whoever did this. But, Mac found your cell phone and called me. I called 911 and Will. Will stayed with you until the paramedics took you and then he piled poor Karma into the back of his sedan and drove him to the emergency vet. Will was pretty riled up. I'm sure he'll be here after awhile. He's been here every day."

I tried to remember the car, any detail about it but all I could recall was the lights and the smoke from the tires.

"Your back pack and phone are in the drawer there." She pointed to the nightstand.

"Thanks, Frankie." I stretched out my legs under the sheets. So stiff.

"Who in the world would try to run down a woman and a dog?"

"I think it's someone who wants me to stop looking into Mad Dog's death. I got a message spray painted on the boutique window one night that told me to stop meddling."

Frankie stared at me wide eyed. "Someone threatened you?"

"Yes. Now I'm really convinced that Hops isn't the killer."

I was having a hard time keeping my eyes open and the sadness was too heavy to fight. Tears spilled down my cheeks.

"Oh, darlin', don't you worry. We'll figure out who's behind this and Karma's going to be just fine. He's a strong boy. You'll see." I felt her hand squeeze mine as I slipped back into the void.

***

Consciousness came again when I heard the door squeak open.

"Is it still Saturday?"

"Yes. It's seven o'clock." It took me a few groggy minutes to realize it wasn't the nurse in the room with me. It was Will. I blinked and let the fuzziness clear.

"Hi."

"Hi." He bent down and planted a light kiss on my forehead. He smelled so good, like the fresh outside air. I breathed him in. He took a seat in the chair Frankie had left by the side of my bed. "How are you?"

"I hear I'll live. Thank you for taking Karma to the vet."

He nodded. "I went by to see him today. I wasn't sure he was going to make it, honestly.

But, he had his eyes opened today. They said he's a fighter."

"Did he wag his tail?"

"No, but he's on some pretty heavy pain killers." He shifted in the chair to lean forward and take my hand. "Did you see the car that hit you?"

"Just the headlights. It was already dark and it happened so fast. I couldn't even comprehend that this car was coming at us... on purpose. But they did. They were waiting down at the dead end and came at us like they wanted to kill us. Karma broke loose and ran straight for it and I ran after him."

"You think this had something to do with the threat left on the window?"

"It's the only logical explanation. I don't think I've made any enemies at the pet boutique."

"But why would they think you were still looking into Mr. Fowler's death?"

"I don't know." Okay, so I lied. I did know. I had mentioned on the yacht that I didn't believe Hops killed Mad Dog. Mac had shaken his head in warning and I didn't listen. But, I didn't have the energy to fight with Will right now.

"You'll have to sign a statement about what you remember. And when you get out of here, you'll need to stay close to home until we can figure out who's behind this attack.

"Okay." Time for a change of subject. "Do you think you could scrounge up a fruit smoothie in this place?"

"Of course." He smiled. "Be right back, don't go anywhere."

"Ha ha." I was drained and once again feeling the allure of the darkness. I had to get out of here. I had to see Karma. I had a boutique to run. And I still had a murder to solve.

THIRTY-FOUR

I slid gingerly into Frankie's little red sports car. "Thanks for driving me, Frankie." It was Tuesday morning and they had finally discharged me with a prescription for Vicodin and a suggestion I take the week off to rest. About now I was wishing I hadn't been so stubborn about bringing some things to St. Pete from Savannah. I could have used a little magick to heal. Guess it was going to be the traditional medicine route for me.

"Sure, sugar. Glad to help. I'm sure seeing you will cheer Karma up. Knowing that you're okay and haven't left him, too."

I readjusted in the leather seat to keep the pressure off of my tender right side. "I hope you're right."

The Emergency Clinic smelled like the hospital plus musky animals. My head reeled and I lost my balance. Frankie caught my arm and led me to the reception window. "Sorry," I whispered. "Still feeling weak."

She patted my arm and smiled at the woman at the desk. "Hi, we're here to see Karma. This is his owner, Darwin Winters."

"Certainly, please have a seat and I'll let them know you're here."

I leaned back in the chair. I couldn't believe how much energy it took just to sit upright. Luckily, it didn't take long for the door to open and a young girl to escort me to the room Karma had called home for the last few days. Frankie waited for me in the lobby.

"Karma!" I fell down on my knees in front of him, taking in his injuries. He looked comfortable enough, stretched out on a cot, but a large bandage covered his chest and his right front leg was in a cast; an IV line stuck out of his other leg. He also had numerous spots that were shaved and sported heavy black stitching. I held my hands over my mouth. It was such a shock to see him like this. "Hey, boy." I wiped at my eyes. His eyes were still closed.

"Hi, Miss Winters." A woman's voice came from behind me. I turned, looked up and shook her hand.

"You must be Dr. Messing?" She nodded. "How is he today?"

"Well, his liver enzymes are high but I think we can just attribute that to the trauma his body has taken. The lacerations and broken bones will take time to heal but I think we can consider him stable as long as we keep the infections at bay."

I stared at his shallow breathing. "Does he know I'm here?"

"He's on some pretty heavy pain killers but on some level he probably does."

Was she just trying to make me feel better? "He's got another week here at least, but you're welcome to visit him once a day and when he's ready to go home, we'll instruct you how to administer the fluids."

"Okay. Thank you."

"Any other questions just have my tech find me, Miss Winters."

She slipped out and left me staring at Karma. The reality of our situation hit me, seeing him so injured and close to death. Someone out there really tried to kill us. Well, probably tried to kill me, Karma just happened to get in the way.

A cold chill gripped me. I was in over my head. I couldn't get help from Will, not unless I was willing to spill all the things I'd been hiding from him. But if I stopped trying to find Mad Dog's killer now, then that person would have gotten away with murder. And I would always be looking over my shoulder, waiting for someone to run me down. Maybe it was time to come clean with Will? I sighed and reached out to rest my hand gingerly on Karma's head.

As my hand touched his warm fur, a white starburst engulfed my mind and shot me full of heat. Within the space of the white energy, an image crystallized. It was the car. A black sports car sporting a gold plate on the front with the words: ON THE MONEY.

I fell back, choking on the smell of burning rubber and smoke. My head pounding, my body buzzing, I stood up and jogged in place—which wasn't easy considering my weakened state. But, if I didn't get the energy from the vision released in a slow, consistent manner, it would release itself in a flash of destruction. I almost had it under control but didn't quite have enough oomph to keep going. I felt the release as a light bulb popped and rained down on me. I collapsed to the floor, my hair soaked in sweat, trying to catch my breath and burn the image of the car in my mind.

Eventually, the smell dissipated and I was calm enough to scoot back over to Karma. I kissed the side of his nose and stroked his ear. "I got it, boy. Thank you." His eyes opened slightly and his tail thumped three times on the cot. It was the most joyful sound in the world to me. I laughed and wiped my face on my shirt. "Yeah, you know I'm here, don't you? That's right. Neither one of us are going anywhere." I rested my cheek on his and listened to his breathing.

On the ride home, I gave Will a call and told him I remembered something about the car that ran us down.

THIRTY-FIVE

The next few days were a Vicodin induced blur. I tried not to take the pain killers but then couldn't function at the boutique. Every muscle in my body screamed at me. Will came to check on me one morning, but he was on an undercover investigation that was keeping him busy.

Sylvia spent a lot of her time making sure I had eaten and wasn't on my feet too long. On Thursday, she even made me go upstairs and take a nap at lunchtime, which I frankly welcomed.

The exhaustion of just trying to talk was overwhelming and everyone wanted to hear the story. Karma's empty bed behind the counter was a constant reminder of his absence and by Friday, I broke down and cried for an hour in the storage room.

After that, I did feel better. Emotionally, anyway. The physical feeling that I'd been hit by a train kept right on trucking.

On Saturday, I slept in and then took a cab to visit Karma. His eyes were open when I went in the room and his tail began to thump immediately. I grinned big and smothered him with kisses and careful hugs.

Now that all my energy wasn't consumed with his survival, since the vet considered the threat of infection gone, I got back to thinking about the killer. I was tired of playing games.

I gave the cab driver the address to the town house.

Unfortunately, pounding on the door for ten minutes led to nothing. No one was there. I walked home, frustrated and aching.

I slid my card in the gate and then turned as I heard someone approach me from behind. My heart raced but it was just Mac.

"Hey, Snow White, how you feelin'?"

"Hey, Mac." I crossed my arms and smiled. "Doing better. Surprised to see you here. Are you checking on me?"

He glanced around. "Can we talk a minute?"

I motioned toward the open gate. "You want to come up?"

"Naw," he fidgeted with his hat. "I prefer to stay out here."

"Okay, want a cup of tea?"

"All right."

We sat outside the Hooker Tea Company, each with a cold tea. Even under the shade, it was a sweltering afternoon. "So, what's up?"

"We all feel real bad about you and Karma almost gettin' killed. It's just way out of hand, all this mess. You shouldn't be involved." He dropped his head and then looked back up at me, his brown eyes rimmed with red. "We're gonna take care of it, find out who drove that car and turn 'em in."

"Mac, if you know something, just tell me."

"No. Like I said, you shouldn't be involved."

I watched a small lady walk by with two Great Danes. It made me miss Karma. "Okay, here's what I know. The car was a black sports car with a gold plate that said ON THE MONEY. You know who drives that?"

"Never seen it before but that helps. I'll let you know when we find 'em. Meanwhile, lay low, will ya? I know Mad Dog would be mad as hell if we let something happen to you. So, you officially have our help."

I actually was touched. It was nice someone was willing to step up. "Okay. Thank you." When Mac nodded and got up, I added, "Y'all be careful. This isn't a nice person we're dealing with."

He grinned. "Don't you worry. We're not all that nice, either."

THIRTY-SIX

I stepped outside the boutique after a quiet Monday, looking forward to a long bath and an early bedtime. It was odd not having to walk Karma across the street. I missed him. As I was locking up, I heard someone call my name.

"Darwin!" Frankie was waving from her little red sports car, wearing a matching red straw hat.

I walked over. "Hey, Frankie. Nice night for a drive."

"Yes, it is," her voice wavered. "And I was hoping I could talk you into coming on one with me?"

"Oh, I don't know, I'm pretty beat."

"Pretty please, sugar... I... I really need a friend right now."

"Everything okay?"

"I don't know. I found Maddy. I mean, I hired a private detective and he found Maddy. She's living in an apartment downtown. I want to go talk to her, make sure she's okay but I don't want to go alone. Will you come?"

"Sure." I walked around to the passenger side and slid in, patting Frankie's knee. "Heaven knows I understand the need for closure."

Her smile widened, exposing her perfect teeth with the smear of red lipstick. I smiled, too.

We drove out of the Beach Drive district, through the rougher parts of St. Pete that hadn't been given a multi-million dollar facelift. I liked being in the convertible with the wind and sounds of evening swirling around us. Lifting my arms up, I wiggled my fingers in the cool air current. Maybe I would learn to drive one day and have a convertible.

Frankie didn't seem to notice my enchantment with her car. "How's Karma doin'?"

"Good. Well, better. Dr. Messing says I can probably bring him home at the end of the week."

"Oh, that's great news. Poor dog. Been through enough. Just burns my britches that someone would try to hurt him... and you of course." She was shaking her head and slowing down. "There. That's the apartments."

She pulled into a guest parking space and shut off the car. "Ready?"

"Ready."

We made our way through a lobby full of wicker furniture and ceiling fans to the elevator.

"It's number 704." Frankie was quiet on the way up. She looked worried.

"You really care about her, don't you?"

"God knows why, she's hell on wheels, but yeah, I do."

I squeezed Frankie's hand. "You're doing the right thing. I'm sure you can clear up whatever's going on."

We stepped off the elevator and found the door with a brass 704. Frankie took a deep breath, blew it out then knocked. I stood a few feet away, against the wall. I would be there for support if she needed me, but I didn't want to intrude on their conversation.

A few tense moments ticked by and Frankie knocked again. I was beginning to think Maddy wasn't home when the door finally clicked open.

Maddy's profile appeared in the door way. Her hair was pulled back in a tight ponytail and her expression was anything but friendly. I looked her over, a feeling of dread making my head tingle. Was she...?

"What are you doing here, Frankie?"

"Well, is that anyway to greet a friend? I was worried about you." Frankie noticed then, too. She stared at the slight bulge under Maddy's tight tank top. "Holy hades, are you pregnant?"

"Not really your concern. You need to leave."

Frankie stiffened her shoulders. "I... I can help you. I want to help you, Maddy. Please, tell me what's going on."

"Vick." I didn't mean to say it out loud. Maddy turned then, noticing me for the first time. Her face paled and her eyes darkened. Well, the cat was out of the bag now. "It's Vick's baby, isn't it?"

Frankie was glancing from me to Maddy. Her hands had dropped to her sides; her voice had dropped to a whisper. "Maddy, is that true?"

Maddy came at me then, surprisingly fast for a woman with another human being in her belly, and shoved me hard to the ground. Spit flew from her mouth as she kicked and screamed at me.

"You just can't mind your own business!" And some other explosive words that I barely caught, as I was busy trying to scoot back out of the way of her wrath. She managed to connect a hard kick to my bruised right ribs and I yelped in pain. She lost her balance and fell on top of me. We rolled around. I managed to get my knees between us and pushed hard against her as she grabbed my hair.

Frankie came to my rescue once the initial shock wore off. She grabbed Maddy's arms, yanked her up and pinned her against the wall. I sat, panting and shaking, on the ground.

"Enough!" Frankie's tough street persona was now in the house. "Darwin has nothing to do with this. And you're going to hurt the baby acting like some maniac. Calm down!"

Maddy struggled for a moment then fell silent. "Fine. Let go."

Frankie slowly released her then she helped me off the ground and we walked back to the elevator, both of us shaking.

"Stay away from me!" Maddy shouted. She slammed the door. I closed my eyes and leaned against the elevator wall. My right side throbbed as I made an effort to slow down my breathing.

"I'm so stupid," Frankie said, the words releasing sobs that wracked her body as we rode back down to the lobby.

I slipped an arm around her. "It's not stupid to care about people." I couldn't even imagine how this betrayal must be wrecking her inside.

We sat in the parking lot for a while until Frankie could pull herself together enough to drive. I just let her talk, scream and cry. It was exhausting feeling her emotions run amok, taking her from rage to grief and back again. Besides dealing with the waves of heartache coming from her, I was in shock myself. How could they do this to her? She treated Maddy like a daughter, getting her away from her harmful real family and trying to give her a future. Well, Vick I wasn't so shocked about, but still. He must have no feelings at all.

So, this is how people get bitter and stop opening their hearts to each other. Frankie had such a good heart. I didn't want her to close it off to the world just because she picked the wrong guy to trust.

"Frankie, you have so many other people in your life that care about you," I assured her, digging more Kleenex from my straw bag, "and need you. You're too good a person to be with someone who would betray you like this. Better you know now."

She stared out into the parking lot, her face slack. "She's going to have his baby."

"Yes. But, Maddy's right. It's their mess to deal with now. You have to let go."

She nodded and burst out in tears again. I handed her the wad of Kleenex.

It was late by the time she dropped me off and I made her promise not to confront Vick that evening. She needed time to recover, to think about what she needed to say to him. To not kill him on sight.

I hugged her. "Come by in the morning and have tea with me so I know you're okay."

"All right," she sniffed. "I will. Thanks for coming. I don't know what I would have done if I had been by myself."

"You would have been fine. You're a survivor, Frankie. Remember that."

I soaked my sore bones in a hot bath when I got home. The big place was empty and my sadness had pulled me down to new lows. Relationships seemed so complicated, each person having their own needs and motivations. I was suddenly grateful for my long incubation period without having to deal with one. This made me think of Will. Was I even ready for one now at twenty eight? Not if I couldn't be honest with him. I saw the devastation first hand that dishonesty caused. I wasn't doing anything on purpose to hurt him but he would be hurt all the same. I would either have to come clean or let him go.

I let myself slip beneath the soapy water to hide.

THIRTY-SEVEN

Frankie showed up—face puffy, Itty and Bitty in tow—about an hour after we opened the next morning. Sylvia rushed over to her with open arms, the Portuguese flying.

"*Não posso crer a. What um idiota!*"

Frankie accepted the hug and gave me a small smile over her shoulder. "I take it Sylvia knows?"

I nodded and took out some fresh peanut butter biscuits for the pups. "How are you this morning?"

"I'm better. And, I've decided, probably better off." She took the biscuits and bent down to offer them to the Chihuahuas.

"That's right, Frankie." Sylvia had been riled up since I told her what happened this morning. She was definitely not someone I'd want to betray. She shook her head, her sleek ponytail flying back and forth. "Have people gone mad? I just don't understand. It's like the devil himself is in town."

"Yeah, well, maybe he is. I tried to call Vick this morning. Of course he's not answering his phone. Maddy probably called him as soon as we left last night."

"Gah! I go to Cassis. We need chocolate croissants." Sylvia grabbed her purse from under the counter and patted Frankie's arm on the way out. "He was not good enough for you anyhow."

"That's why I love Sylvia. Her answer to every crisis is pastries." I went over and made us both a cup of tea.

"Thanks, sugar." Frankie sipped from her cup. "I guess I need to start lookin' for another assistant. I was holding out hope that I could talk some sense into Maddy and she'd come back. I'm gonna pack up all Vick's crap out of my condo, too and leave it on his front lawn." Her lip began to quiver. "Maybe set it on fire."

I laughed then said, "Welcome to Darwin's," as a new customer walked in. "Let me know if I can help you with anything." I turned back to Frankie. "I have an idea. Why don't you let me keep Itty and Bitty for a few days and you take off. Go on a cruise or pamper yourself at a spa."

"Oh, I don't know."

"It'll be good for you. And it's pretty lonely upstairs without Karma. He doesn't come home until Friday. They girls can keep me company until then."

Frankie thought about it and began to nod. "You know what? You're right. Getting away is probably a good idea. Yeah. Okay. Thanks, Darwin."

Sylvia buzzed back in with a bakery box that smelled like heaven. As she and Frankie dug in and chatted, I walked to the back to check on the new customer. The bells jingled while I was back there and I heard Sylvia call my name.

After I answered the customer's questions about our organic cat food, I walked back up front.

Will stood there, looking all official in his suit and all sweet and inviting at the same time. My heart flip-flopped like a fish out of water. I groaned and melted, hating myself for not being stronger.

I couldn't do much but smile up at him. "Hey, Will."

"Hi. Good to see you up and around." He gave me a light hug, his bright eyes flashing. "How are you feeling?"

"I'm fine. What's up?"

He slid some pictures out of a brown envelope he had been holding. "I need you to take a look at these and tell me if this is the car that ran you down."

"Sure." I took the pictures and nodded. Black sports car, one of those older muscle cars with a gold front 'ON THE MONEY' plate. "Yes. This is it. You found it? Who owns it?"

He took the photos and slipped them back in the envelope. "The owners live in Tampa but this Camaro was reported stolen two weeks ago. We picked up some punk kids joy riding around in it, who said they found it abandoned at the beach with the keys in the ignition. They all have alibis for the night you were hit. We're pulling prints, but with so many people in and out of it now, it's going to be tough to get clean ones." He must have seen the disappointment in my face. He rubbed my arm gently. "Hey, it's a miracle you remembered the car at all, being so dark and it happening so fast. Let's just be grateful about that for now and we'll work on the other stuff, okay?"

I let myself look into his eyes. So trusting. This was it. Let him go? The thought was a physical pain in my chest. No. Come clean.

"Yeah, about that, Will. I need to talk to you about something. Are you free tonight?"

He looked worried. "I've got three late nights coming up. Is it important? Can it wait until Friday night?"

"Oh, sure." I waved it off. "Not really important. Just something I need to share with you."

"Okay." He glanced around and then leaned down and kissed me. "Dinner then. I'll call you."

When he left, I joined Frankie in choking down my misery with a chocolate croissant.

THIRTY-EIGHT

Thursday evening I busied myself baking some carob and peanut butter cupcakes, both for the boutique and for Karma's coming home welcome tomorrow. Itty and Bitty were sitting attentively in the kitchen, taking turns yapping at me as I used melted, colored yogurt to decorate the cupcake tops with blue and pink paw prints and bones.

"Don't worry, girls, you'll get one." I kneeled down and let them lick the spatula with their postage stamp tongues. They really had been great company but Frankie was picking them up around eight tonight. I hoped the time away had allowed her to come to terms with her situation and heal some.

My cell phone began to vibrate on the counter. I wiped my hands on my apron. "Hello?"

"Hi, Darwin?"

"Yes?"

"This is Betsy Mills. You had asked me about a townhouse on Fifth Avenue?"

"Oh! Yes."

"I have that information for you. It's owned by a corporation, but I do remember making that

262 | Shannon Esposito

sale to Vick Bruno. You would have met him at the homeless benefit... he's Frankie's boyfriend."

Whoa! Vick? All kinds of things were running through my mind. Did Vick kill Mad Dog there? But Frankie said he was with her that night. Was she just giving him an alibi?

"Hello? Darwin, are you there?"

"Yes... yes... thank you. I do know Mr. Bruno. I really appreciate you giving me a call back on this. Next time you come in, your poodles can have a gourmet treat on me."

"Glad to help. See you soon."

I hung up and stood at the counter, stunned. Then I shuffled into the living room like a zombie and cracked my shin on the coffee table.

"Ow!" As I rubbed it, Itty and Bitty trotted over to see what all the fuss was about. I sat on the edge of the couch, staring out the French doors and rubbing their little heads absentmindedly.

Mad Dog had warned me to stay away from Vick, so he did know him. But Vick had an alibi. What about the twins? They had a key to the townhouse. Could they have killed Mad Dog and dumped his body? I couldn't imagine Mad Dog not being able to handle two girls. He certainly could have protected himself from them. I had to go back to the townhouse and find out what was going on there and who was involved. I had run out of options.

I buzzed Frankie up an hour later and hugged her as she came in.

"Well, you look like a new woman," I teased.

"I am." She bent down to greet Itty and Bitty, who were whining and jumping up at her knees. "Did you miss Mommy?" She smiled as they licked her face and ears ferociously. "Okay, okay. Let Momma get in the door."

"You want something to drink? Some hot tea or wine?" I didn't want her rushing off. We needed to talk.

"Some hot tea sounds wonderful." She plopped her purse down on the bar and moved into the living room, the pups at her heels. As she sank into the couch, she said, "You have to go with me to the spa for a weekend soon, Darwin. It really helps you slough off all the garbage in your mind and body. I do feel like a new woman."

I carried the teacups into the living room and set them on the coffee table. "It was a successful getaway then?"

"Oh yeah, I got to thinkin' about a lot of things and ya know... I couldn't think of one darn thing that Vick added to my life. Well, besides... you know... but heck, I could pay for that and not have to deal with the misery of a relationship."

"Frankie!" I laughed, taking a seat beside her. "There's plenty of nice men out there, you just have to pick the right one. But, speaking of Vick..." I couldn't think of any other way to tell her than just straight out. "There's a townhouse on Fifth Avenue I've been watching, trying to figure out what's going on there because I think it's somehow connected to Mad Dog's death." I noticed Frankie's eyes wrinkle with concern. "I asked Betsy Mills to check into it for me, find out who owned it."

"Vick does." Frankie was nodding. "Or rather his company does."

"So you know about it? What does he use it for? He's obviously not living there."

Frankie dropped her head and blew out a deep breath. Then she looked me right in the eyes. "He makes porn movies there and sells them online."

I laughed at first. I thought she was joking. Then when I saw she was dead serious, I sat very still, trying to imagine Mad Dog involved in making porn movies. No, that just didn't make sense. "Is that even legal?"

"Yes. It's legal... not the highest profession, I know. Lord knows I can't judge anybody for their lifestyle though and I didn't judge Vick for his. But, I have never told anybody what he does. Guess that says something different about me judging him, huh?"

I held up my hand. "I won't mention it to anybody, don't worry." As long as that's all that is going on there. I tried to fit this new information in place. "So, I saw the twins, Tammy and Tonya, go in there one night. Are they involved in making these videos too?"

"Yep, I didn't find that out until that night I met you at Landon's magic show." Frankie shook her head and picked up one of the pups. As she stroked it, she was lost in thought. "There's something not quite right about those girls. They seem nice and all... just reckless, I guess."

"What about Landon? Does he know what they're doing?"

"Probably not."

"Frankie, you said that Vick was with you the night that Mad Dog got killed? You're absolutely positive that he didn't sneak out of your place? That he remained there the entire night?"

"Oh yeah, I'm sure."

Well that just left the twins, then. Unless someone else had access to the house. How in the world was I going to find that out?

THIRTY-NINE

Frankie picked me up Friday at lunch time from the boutique to go get Karma. I was so excited I almost didn't notice Frankie's new deep red hair color. Luckily, it was impossible to miss in the sunlight.

"Hey, I like the new do." I slid into her sports car and dug sunglasses out of my bag.

"Thanks, had it done this morning. Figure if I'm gonna attract a different type of fish, I need to use a different kind of bait."

We laughed together. I was glad to see she had recovered so quickly. I hoped Karma could get his spirits back quickly, too.

She introduced me to country music at obscene decibels as we drove to the Emergency Vet Clinic. My ears were still ringing as we sat in the plastic waiting room chairs.

Eventually, the door opened and the vet tech led Karma through the door.

A mixture of emotions tumbled around inside me. I was glad to see him up and about but his obvious discomfort squeezed my heart. He moved slowly, limping and panting, but his tail was wagging. That was a good sign. I kneeled down in front of him.

"Are you ready to go home, Karma?" Looking into those soft brown eyes, I smiled and kissed his nose. "Whew, you need a bath!"

I paid the enormous vet bill, got a bag full of the stuff I'd need to give him fluids at home and instructions, then Frankie helped me get him settled on the blanket in the tiny back seat. I was glad the convertible top was down, I couldn't imagine being confined to a tight space with Karma smelling so badly. I'd have to get Sylvia to work her magic on him.

Luckily, I didn't have to wait too long. Sylvia took one whiff of him and squeezed him in between her furry clients, scrubbing him until he smelled like a flower garden.

"Much better," she said, assessing him as he stretched out on his pillow afterwards and happily watched us.

"He looks like he's smiling, doesn't he?" I put a peanut butter cupcake in front of him. He licked at it with his massive tongue.

"I'm sure he didn't like to smell himself, either." Sylvia answered. "Oy! Those cupcakes look good enough for humans!"

I waggled my eyebrows at her. "All natural ingredients."

"I'll stick with Cassis," she laughed and then turned to ring up a gentleman with a schnauzer. "*Alô*, you find everything okay?"

Now that I had Karma back safe and sound, I began to work on the problem of how to find out who was in the townhouse the night Mad Dog died. I couldn't think of any other way to do that besides confront the twins and see how they reacted.

I checked my watch. It was almost closing time. I was supposed to meet Will for dinner at seven, which brought up a whole different set of issues. How was he going to respond to hearing I get psychic images from animals? And that I've been keeping this from him the whole time? Not to mention my family's weirdness—which, I probably wouldn't. My stomach twisted. I pushed these thoughts away. Finding Mad Dog's killer had to stay a priority.

I only had an hour to stop by the townhouse and see if the twins were there. If not, I would go by Landon's magic show after my dinner with Will and talk to them there. Maybe Will would go with me? Stop it, Darwin! Happily ever after is dangerous territory to go fantasizing in.

I took a quick shower, gave Karma his fluids, blocked off the stairs and made a pillow bed on the living room floor for him so he didn't try to climb up to the bedroom with his broken leg.

"Okay, you hold down the fort, Karma. I have to go back to the townhouse tonight." I scratched under his ears. "I'm getting close to finding out what really happened to Mad Dog. You rest and I'll be back later." I kissed him between the eyes hoping he could understand me. Hoping he would know when it was over. Hoping he would understand somehow when the mystery was solved and justice was done.

I maneuvered my bike down the sidewalk to the townhouse, dropping it in the grass before I walked up to the front door. A light was on behind the heavy curtain and I could hear voices inside, arguing. I suddenly wasn't so confident with my decision to just waltz up and knock. I should see who I'd be dealing with first. Stepping back off the porch, I snuck around the side, through the weeds and peered through the window on the back door. The kitchen light burned bright and I could see shadows beyond that but still didn't know if the twins were in there. I wiggled the knob. Locked.

The footsteps behind me barely registered before a blow to the back of my head knocked me to my knees and then into the land of unconsciousness.

FORTY

I heard voices as I came to. Where was I? It all came flooding back with a force that made my head throb. Well, my wish had been granted... I was now inside the townhouse. I tried to move my arms, but my hands were tied behind my back and almost too numb to feel.

Forcing my eyes open, I saw light seeping in beneath the closed door. Someone's hysterical scream startled me. I strained to hear the conversation.

"You have to calm down! Shit, I can't hear myself think!"

I recognized that voice. It was Vick.

"It's over. You have to turn yourselves in."

That was Mac's voice! Mac was here, thank heavens. I tried to scream through the cloth gag in my mouth. Too muffled. He knew I was in here, right? I squirmed to get my legs, which were also tied, to maneuver me upright. Youch! A rabbit was kicking the inside of my skull. Gritting my teeth, I bore the pain and pulled myself into a seated position. I waited for the wave of nausea to pass and then tried to stand on my bound feet. I crashed back onto the mattress. Who would think this would be so hard?

Vick's voice now rose over a female's crying. Mac was shouting back.

"Mac!" I screamed. No use. He couldn't hear me. I had to get to the door.

Suddenly, there was a sound like *ptwhew*! A heavy thud and the female yelped.

Then silence.

I held my breath, my own heartbeat thumped in my ears. I sat there, not knowing what to do. Mac? I didn't hear his voice anymore. As I stared at the closed door and the shouting resumed, I suddenly realized just how much danger I was in. No one knew where I was. I thought about Karma waiting for me at home and about Will waiting for me at dinner. Would he think I stood him up and just go home? If I didn't show up at the boutique in the morning, would Sylvia call the police? By then it would be too late.

I couldn't wait until morning. I knew I wouldn't survive the night in this place.

The door suddenly burst open and Vick stared down at me holding a gun with some kind of long black tube on the end. "You." He waved the gun at me and I couldn't tear my eyes from it. "If you would have minded your own damned business about Mad Dog's death..." Reaching down, he grabbed the back of my arm and pulled me up off the mattress. I tried to fight him, but his fingers dug into my flesh. "Come on, I want to show you what you've done."

The scene in that little living room wiped away all hope of getting out of there alive.

Mac lay on the floor, face down, blood pooling on the hardwood floor beneath his torso. I lunged toward him, tears streaming down my face. Vick held me tight. He dragged me over to an upright punching bag. Forcing me against it, he yelled at the woman standing there glaring at me. "Get the rope!"

It was Maddy!

She didn't look good. Mascara ran in thick streaks down her face.

"Shit," she slurred, still crying. Obviously high on something, she stumbled over to the box and pulled out rope. She brought it back and held it out to Vick.

As he wound the rope around me, tethering me to the punching bag, Maddy glared at me, her sobs coming out as hiccups.

"You have ruined everything!" She fell forward with the force of her anger. Gaining her balance, she balled her hands into fists. "You made me lose my baby!"

My heart lurched. I hoped that wasn't true. I needed to be able to talk to her, try to reason with her but the cloth stuffed in my mouth prevented that. The only thing I could do was shake my head vigorously.

"Yes! Yes, you did." She swung at me, her knuckles connecting with the bottom of my chin. It hurt but could have been worse. I squeezed my eyes shut, waiting for her to hit me again.

"Whoa," Vick said. "There'll be plenty of time for that. Wait 'til the video's rollin' darlin'."

My eyes flew open. Plenty of time? Video? Oh, this wasn't good.

Vick finished tethering me to the punching bag and stepped back. His dark eyes bore into mine. He reached over and pulled the cloth from my mouth.

I took a deep breath and moved my jaw around. "Please, I didn't mean to--"

"Shut your mouth!" Maddy screamed.

Vick grabbed her around the waist as she lunged toward me again.

"You shut your mouth," Maddy choked. "You're the one who should be dead. Not my baby."

"It's all right, Maddy. You'll get your revenge." Vick grinned at me. "You messed with the wrong girl, honey."

My head was pounding and I was freaking out. I watched in horror as Maddy stumbled back to the box and pulled out a pair of leather gloves with metal spikes sticking out of the knuckles. As she came toward me, pulling them on, I thought of my mother and sisters. Who would tell them what happened to me? Will they know that I loved them, even as I had to leave them? I closed my eyes as Vick stepped behind a video camera and yelled, "Showtime!"

FORTY-ONE

The first blow was to my chest. It knocked the wind out of me and the spikes stung as they penetrated my skin. I braved a look into her eyes as she wound up for another punch. What I saw there was pure rage... maybe madness. Whatever part of her that had been human, that could have prevented her from killing me, was gone. The single-mindedness of her hatred terrified me. Nothing I could say would stop her. So, I closed my eyes and tried to put myself as far away from my physical being as possible. I went back home in my mind, to Savannah.

My sisters were gathered in the kitchen. They smiled at me as I entered and I rushed into their arms.

The second blow was to my head. It felt like a boulder crashed into me and the shocking pain pulled me back to the townhouse. I felt the spikes tear through the flesh of my cheek. Tiny black dots danced in my vision. I decided it was better to keep my eyes open, if I could, and know when the next blow was coming.

How long would I stay conscious during a beating like this? I felt the blood, wet and sticky, running down my face and into my shirt. I hoped the next blow would knock me out.

"This video is going to be gold, darlin'!" Vick said, laughing.

In the back of my mind, Vick's words disturbed something deep within me. I reached for the questions that now rose like sediment floating impossibly upward toward the surface. "Video?" I managed to push the word out on borrowed breath.

Maddy swayed in front of me, grinning but let her arms drop. "Oh, yeah. You're gonna be an internet star just like your friend, Mad Dog."

"Shut up, Maddy! Just keep workin' her."

"No," she whirled around to face Vick. "It doesn't matter if she knows now. She can take it to the grave with her." She turned slowly back to me and put her face inches from mine. I could smell her sweat mixed with alcohol. "I didn't mean to kill Mad Dog. I liked him, actually. We were shooting the video and us girls had been drinkin'. Tonya said, 'Hey, I dare you to use the new brass knuckles.' Maddy swayed and fell back, laughing and shrugged. "Why not?"

Tears were streaming down my face, mingling with the blood. The salty mixture filled my mouth. Maddy killed Mad Dog? But why didn't he stop her? Was he tied up like this? The thought made me sick to my stomach. I dropped my head.

"Yep, so now you know. We panicked and dumped him at the lake. Tried to make it look like he just got drunk and drowned."

"With my good rum," Vick threw in.

"Oops." Maddy laughed then shifted back into psycho mode. "But no... you just couldn't let it be. Probably dump your nosey ass there, too."

It was truly over. I knew the truth but I wouldn't be able to tell anyone. Maddy would get away with it. The best I could hope for was my death would lead Will to investigate further and maybe they would uncover the truth then.

I'm so sorry, Karma. I pictured him in my mind and tried to send him a last goodbye. I could almost hear his deep bark.

Suddenly, the door shook as someone pounded on it.

My head snapped up. Maddy whirled around and shared a concerned look with Vick.

The knocking stopped and then the door crashed in. I saw Vick drop to the floor and go for the gun he had left there. Maddy bolted for the back door, jumping over Mac's body, tripping then stumbling back up.

Will and three other officers pushed into the room, guns out, yelling, "Police, freeze!"

A large brown mass pushed by them and tackled Maddy in the hallway with a loud thud.

Karma!

"Get off me!" She screamed. One of the officers grabbed her arms and cuffed her. Another officer wrestled Vick to the ground, knocking over the video camera. The third one checked Mac's vitals. "He's alive. I'll call it in."

Karma limped over to me and began sniffing me with abandon, his tail wagging. Will was right behind him.

"Oh my god," he whispered as he saw my face. He worked quickly to untie me and I collapsed in his arms. All the pain was a tidal wave rushing in now. I whimpered as Will helped me to sit on the floor. Karma pushed in next to me, resting a large paw on my leg. "Hang on. The paramedics will be here soon."

I squinted at Will through my swollen eye lid and tried to smile, but the tears just spilled out faster. "Maddy killed Mad Dog. She confessed. They videotaped it."

Will reached out and held his palm to the side of my face that wasn't beat to a bloody pulp. "We've got her. We'll sort it out, don't worry. I'm sorry I didn't believe you, Darwin."

I glanced up as the officers escorted Maddy and Vick out. "How did you find me?"

"Karma." Will patted his flanks affectionately. "I got worried when you didn't show up at dinner, with someone threatening you and then running you down in a car... so I had Sylvia let me in your place when you didn't answer. Karma was frantic. We let him out and he led us here. When I saw your bike in the grass, I knew you were in trouble."

Dizziness rushed in as I turned my head. Karma couldn't save Mad Dog, but he saved me. How did he know? I closed my eyes as Will instructed the paramedics who had arrived. Maybe the visions were more like a connection, a two way exchange of energy? Will reluctantly let me go as two gentle hands took over.

Good boy.

FORTY-TWO

Three days later, I was back at the boutique, enjoying a cup of tea and feeling lighter than I had in months, despite my new injuries. It was already a gorgeous St. Pete morning, full of sunshine and possibility. Or maybe it was just the fact that I had survived? There's something precious about each new morning after you thought you'd never see one again.

Sylvia and Frankie were hanging out with me. We were all thanking our lucky stars we lived through the threat Vick and Maddy had posed in our lives. Even Mac had survived. He would be in the hospital recovering for awhile but he wasn't complaining about the soft bed, hot food or cute nurses.

I adjusted my sore bones on the chair in front of the window, letting the sunshine warm the side of my face not covered in bandages.

"I still can't believe it was Maddy who killed Mad Dog," Frankie said. "I guess you never really know somebody."

"Shocking, yeah. But so is the fact those three girls were involved in such a barbaric activity to begin with," I said.

"*Sim é demente*," Sylvia sighed. "Landon must now find new assistants. *Demente meninas.* So," her brow furrowed, "they would pay the homeless people for these girls to beat them up? And sell the videos? Who would buy such a thing?"

"Not just that," I said, "but Vick had a hidden page that you could only shop on after he charged five thousand dollars on your credit card. Will said it was real sick stuff, including the video of Mad Dog's death."

I still couldn't digest this part. Yeah, Vick deserved to be locked up, but what about all the people buying this kind of violence? Supporting it? Do they just get to walk away?

"So, Vick wrote the suicide note and forced Junior to turn it in?" Frankie asked.

"Yep."

"I can't believe I didn't see what a scumbag he really was," Frankie said.

We all sat sipping our tea for a moment. It was all so surreal.

"Was it Vick who tried to run you over then?" Sylvia asked.

"Nope, Will said it was Maddy. She apparently got the car from her brother, who stole it in Tampa. I guess Vick told her I was still suspicious of Mad Dog's death and she decided she needed to cover her tracks." I didn't mention the part where I confronted Vick on the yacht with the words 'I know about Maddy.' He must've thought I was talking about her killing Mad Dog.

"You could have gotten yourself killed," Sylvia scolded me, then made the sign of the cross.

"Yeah," Frankie said, "but she didn't, thank the Lord. And they would've all got away with it and kept hurting people. You did the right thing, Darwin. Maybe not the smart thing... but the right thing."

"Thanks, Frankie." I laughed and then winced as the stitches in my cheek pulled tight.

"Though Hops is gonna be sore at you for awhile for getting him out of jail," she chuckled.

Just then, the first customers of the day entered the boutique.

"Welcome to Darwin's." Sylvia smiled. "What can we help you *senhoras* with today?"

The woman adjusted her purse on her shoulder. "Hi, are you Darwin?"

"That'd be me," I raised my hand. "Can I help you?"

Her eyes widened at the sight of the bandages covering the side of my face. She put a protective hand on the young girl's shoulder standing next to her.

Karma had gotten up and ambled over on his three good legs to greet them. The young girl kneeled down and slipped her arms around him.

"Wow, he doesn't usually greet people like that." I smiled. "Your daughter must be a real dog person."

"Yes. She's been begging me for a dog forever," the woman said. She seemed nervous. "Is he dangerous?"

"No, he's a big love... besides, he doesn't have any teeth."

"Oh, okay." She held out her hand to me. "You left a message on our phone. I'm Nina Fowler." I took her hand, every hair standing up on my arms. "This is Mariah." She nodded down at the girl.

I glanced from her to Mariah and back, my eyes blurring with tears. I stood up and gently hugged her. "Thank you for coming. I know he'd want Mariah to have his sketch book. Follow me."

I walked her to the counter where I had stashed the book. When I held it out to her, she closed her eyes for a moment as her fingers clutched it. I couldn't help but notice she was still wearing her wedding band.

"There's an envelope of money in the back, too. He wrote Mariah's name on it."

She flipped back to the envelope then met my eyes. "Can I ask you how you got this?" Her voice shook. "How did you know him?"

"I only knew him for a week, really. But that was long enough to know he was a good person that deserved better. You knew he was homeless?"

"Yes," she kept her voice low, wiping at a tear that slipped out. "He left us because he was afraid he would hurt us. Not on purpose. But, he was a haunted man. He couldn't be indoors or control the day terrors. What happened? How did he...?"

"That's a long story." I glanced over at Mariah, who was watching us, one arm draped over Karma. "One I'd rather tell you when your daughter isn't around. Can you stay? I've got plenty of room in my townhouse upstairs and I can fill you in on everything tonight. Also, your husband was cremated but the ashes are still in storage. If you'd like, we can give him a proper goodbye. Maybe have a sea burial?"

"Yes," she was holding back sobs now, "I would like that very much and I think it would be good for Mariah to have closure. Thank you."

***

So that's exactly what we did. Frankie worked her own particular kind of magic and chartered us a yacht for the next evening. A different kind of energy brought as all together this time—relief and love and gratitude.

Nina and Mariah got to meet Mad Dog's Pirate City family and we even got G onboard— with the promise of cookies, of course. She shared with us the person Mad Dog was before the war; the kind, sensitive happy family man. I was glad his little girl got to see how much he meant to us all. We had a celebration of Mad Dog's life before we let him go.

At one point on the way back, with the salty breeze and the lights of St. Pete dotting the perimeter of the Bay, Will stood behind me and slipped his arms around me.

"So, what was it you wanted to share with me?"

"Oh." My heart sank. Yeah, that. Did I still need to tell him everything now that the case was solved? I didn't feel up to it, that's for sure. "Nothing important." Maybe another day it would be important, but right now, I didn't want to risk losing this oasis of happiness we had found.

"Okay but you owe me a dinner and an explanation." He squeezed me tighter. "How did you know about that townhouse being connected?"

"Women's intuition." I held onto his arms, his warmth and the moment, burning each into my memory.

***

For the two days Mad Dog's family stayed with me, I noticed Karma never left Mariah's side. I had a decision to make.

We said our goodbyes outside the boutique Wednesday evening and, with a heavy heart, I made the only decision that made sense.

"Nina, I think you should take Karma home with you, for Mariah."

She began to shake her head in protest and I stopped her and turned her around to look at the mastiff with her daughter. Mariah had her arms wrapped around him, her head buried in his fur. "That dog belongs in your family. He attached himself to your husband... and now your daughter. He belongs with her."

I noticed her shoulders fall. Then a mixture of laughter and tears burst through; all the emotions from the past few days pouring out into the universe. "What do you feed a giant, toothless dog?"

I laughed then, too. "Anything from the blender." Then I went and kneeled down in front of the little girl. Mad Dog's little girl. I studied her for a moment in the fading light. She had his eyes and hands. More than that, though, she had his soft spirit. He wasn't gone. He was right here, in front of me, holding onto Karma with different arms, same heart.

"Mariah?"

She looked up at me, eyes rimmed red. "Yes, ma'am?"

"If Karma went home with you, would you promise to take very good care of him?"

Mariah's eyes widened and she glanced at her mother.

"Your mom said it's okay."

A grin slowly lit up her face. "Yes, ma'am!" Then she flung her arms back around Karma, giggling and wiping at her nose.

A wave of joy washed over me, making my scalp tingle. Karma looked up at me, tongue hanging, eyes squinting. Yeah, he was definitely smiling.

I bent down and pressed my cheek against his forehead one last time. "You take good care of

Mariah, boy. I'll miss you." One last kiss and one last smile through the tears.

It was tricky getting Karma up into the jeep with his cast, but the three of us managed and they were finally all packed in, ready to go home. I slipped my hands under Karma's ears. "Thanks for everything, boy. You take good care of your new family now."

His eyes sparkled happily as his tongue licked the tears from the unbandaged side of my face.

I kissed his nose then reached over and slipped a check into Nina's bag. "That's for the vet bills. You come by anytime for a visit and to stock up on more treats, promise?"

"Promise," Nina said. "Thank you, Darwin... for everything."

Sylvia slipped her arm around my shoulder as we watched them pull out onto Beach Drive, their headlights disappearing around the corner. I wiped at my eyes and cheek. I think I slobbered more that day than Karma ever had.

"Come on, we get some chocolate scones," Sylvia said, dabbing a finger under her eye.

I glanced at her. "Sylvia, are you crying?"

"Ack," she waved, "something in my eye."

I slipped my arm through hers. "Yeah, I'll miss the big guy, too."

She sniffed and I heard her say a little prayer as we made our way down the sidewalk, under the streetlights to Cassis.

"Well, I'd say our first few months open have been a success. What do you think?" I asked.

"I think I hope we have continued success with snowbird season but not quite so much adventure."

I threw my head back and laughed at the sky. When I did, I swear a star winked at me.

LADY LUCK RUNS OUT
(Pet Psychic No. 2)

PROLOGUE

Rose Faraday knew it was time to stop ignoring her niggling gut and the metaphorical neon-flashing signs the universe had been manifesting around her. She lowered herself onto the sofa, unwrapped her tarot cards from their silk fabric covering and spread the cloth out on the coffee table. A long-haired, black cat wound itself around her ankle, and then deposited a fake mouse on her foot. "Mew!"

She smiled down into eyes as green and clear as emeralds and sighed. "Not now, Lucky, Mama's got to work." She scratched the cat under the belly with her bare toes and then pushed her gently away, "Go on, we'll play fetch later. Scooch." Lucky squeaked out one more "mew" in protest then sauntered off, hopping through the cat door to the screened lanai, where her favorite scratching post awaited.

Rose took a deep breath, letting the scent of the burning jasmine incense relax her, and closed her eyes. When she felt ready, she opened and took out the time-softened cards, arranging them in three piles on the silk. The mounting feeling of dread had prompted her to read for herself today and she needed to be relaxed. To concentrate on the question: Am I in physical danger?

After shuffling the cards three times, she slid the first one off the pile and laid it down. Ten of Swords. Her least favorite card. Well, things couldn't get worse, that wasn't exactly bad news. She slid the next card off the deck and placed it upright to the left of the Ten of Swords.

The Death Card. Rose stared at the skeletal face in the black armor. So, something was coming to an end? A transformation? She held the question "Am I in physical danger?" in the forefront of her mind. Heaviness fell upon her. She shivered. Then again, sometimes death just meant death.

Rose shook off the thought and pulled a third card, placing it to the right of the Ten of Swords. Judgment reversed. She noted her own reaction to this card, a nervousness that she knew meant the card wasn't just about closing a door on the past and having a new beginning. It was about a decided end.

Defiantly, she pulled a fourth clarifying card and placed it to the right of Judgment.

The Six of Swords. She always subscribed to the belief this card represented Charon, the ferryman who shuttled the departed across the River Styx. With all the other cards preceding this one, it was hard to ignore the possibility she was indeed in physical danger. Her breath grew shallow and she had to force herself to deepen it, to calm her thoughts. Her left hand fluttered to the gold cuff bracelet on her right wrist and began twisting it, as was her habit when she felt anxious. It had been her mother's. The one piece of jewelry that hadn't been buried with her.

Okay. One more clarifying card.

Rose flipped it over and placed it to the left of the Death card.

The Devil. Another dark card. She involuntarily pushed back away from the spread in front of her. Fear wound its way through her body, causing the hair on the back of her neck to prickle. She wiped the sweat from her upper lip.

A crash from the lanai made her jump. She placed a hand on her racing heart. Good gracious! Sounded like Lucky knocked over one of her potted plants again.

"Lucky, leave the lizards alone!" she called. That cat would never learn. She'd deal with the mess later. Right now she had more important things to worry about.

Rose gathered up the cards and wrapped them back up. It was time to consult her crystal ball. With trembling hands, she retrieved it and set it on the coffee table in front of her.

Rose took a few deep breaths to let the turmoil of anxiety sink to the bottom and let her mind clear. Then she began to rub the crystal ball. Its cool surface gave her comfort. Scrying had always been one of her strongest gifts, one of the few useful things her mother had passed down to her.

When she felt calmer and focused, she opened her eyes and stared into the quartz ball, watching light flutter around in its fractured depths. Seconds ticked by, then minutes unnoticed as she continued to hold her focus. A gray mist began to form, swirling and darkening until a black storm raged within the confines of the sphere. Rose's heart fluttered nervously. This was not going to be good news. She visualized the storm disintegrating and watched as the inky, cloudy ball became clear once again.

A serpent sat, coiled tightly, its eyes shifting from black to red. A chill traveled up Rose's arms. She pulled her hands away as if the ball had caught fire.

One hand still resting protectively over her heart, she mulled over the image.

Okay, snakes and their shedding skin symbolize change, releasing old habits. That's what the Devil card must be telling her. She just needed to let go of an old habit. She twisted the bracelet roughly around her arm. Well, crap, she was going to have to give up her pack a day smoking habit. Sure, that made sense. After all, she was fifty-three and had a congenital heart defect, probably pushing her luck, anyway. Didn't take a crystal ball to figure that out.

But, the panic wasn't receding. No matter how she tried to justify the cards and the serpent vision, no matter how hard she tried to push them to the corners of her mind, anxiety fluttered in every cell of her body.

Smoothing out her creased skirt, she nodded. Okay, time to take a break and see what kind of mess her beloved girl made this time. Besides, she could use a quick cuddle. Hearing Lucky's motorboat purr always calmed her nerves.

Rose stood up and took one step. Her right bare foot came down on something cold and hard. She glanced down just in time to register the diamond pattern before a quick strike sent venom coursing through her leg. She squealed, confused, as the diamond back rattler's tail disappeared beneath her sofa. Searing heat radiated up her leg and she fell over onto the sofa, clutching her heart. White hot pain blossomed in her chest, squeezing the breath out of her. She gasped for air.

So, this was it? A literal snake?! Images flashed through her mind. The Devil card grew larger, until she could see the scales on his face, see herself reflected in his beady black eyes. His tongue flicked out at her. She felt so cold. The pain in her chest was unbearable. Her last thought was of her cat. "Lucky, run!"

CPSIA information can be obtained at www.ICGtesting.com
Printed in the USA
LVOW04s1248131015

458064LV00001B/3/P